MASTER FROGS OF THE DOMINION

MASTER FROGS OF THE DOMINION

A Novel

D. R. Bishop

iUniverse, Inc.
New York Lincoln Shanghai

Master Frogs of the Dominion
A Novel

iUniverse, Inc.

For information address:
iUniverse, Inc.
2021 Pine Lake Road, Suite 100
Lincoln, NE 68512
www.iuniverse.com

ISBN: 0-595-27383-1

Printed in the United States of America

Contents

ACKNOWLEDGMENTS

I wish to acknowledge some extraordinary humans. To those whose conversations with me somehow found their way into the story: Thank you. If you think you're one but aren't sure—you are. I want to express special gratitude to Tom Solomon for our work at "the office"; to the Landmark Education Forum Leaders and staff and people who assist for their coaching and training which allowed this story to unfold; to my wonderful friends, Kenny, Tye, Sherdina, Betsy, Tom K, Patricia, Karen, Sean, Kerri, Dona, and David, who read different portions and evolutions of my manuscript and gave their invaluable feedback (I did listen—sometimes); to my family and friends who always support me in everything I do; and most of all to my wife, Jo-Ann, for her love, her creative critiques, and for allowing me to spend all that time in the gorge talking to the frogs.

CHAPTER 1

On the Road

The black shapes of the mountains, stoic against the star-dotted Arizona night sky, made me feel more alone as I drove east along Interstate 40. The car's motor strained in defiance of the sweeping left curve's steep uphill grade. A road sign flew by, illuminated in the headlights, and quickly faded back into the darkness.

A moment later, I saw the sign flash again, this time in my mind—something about frogs up ahead.

I reached over to turn up the radio, its weak AM signal fading in and out like voices drowned out by waves crashing onto a beach. Talk shows usually helped me keep awake, but my thoughts had drifted to the question of what I was doing out there all by myself.

"I want you to go," she had told me. "Find out what you want in your life."

I blinked slowly, thinking about her asking me to go away. What was it that I wanted in my life? Why did she seem to think I was going to find it driving across country by myself? I was pretty sure it wasn't going to be something I'd find in those mountains.

At first, I thought I saw smoke, but I soon realized I had driven into a low cloud. A curtain of dense gray fog had descended over the area. I let up on the accelerator pedal.

I couldn't remember ever seeing that kind of fog in that area before. It was like driving with a dull film on the windows. I could barely make out the line at the right edge of the road. Everything was suddenly all wet.

I hunched over the steering wheel, trying to keep my focus between the trusted white line and the rear-view mirror, fearing some big-rig trucker, in a hurry to drop his load, would plow into the back of me at any moment. It occurred to me that there had been no other traffic for a long time, and I wondered why.

I started remembering tragedies from the past caused by dense fog, the seventy-car pile-ups that seemed to happen every few years back in the San Joaquin Valley, a couple of my own near misses. I tightened my grip on the wheel and drove slowly on, shaking with fear.

Pushing on now a little faster than I should have, around fifteen miles per hour, I began thinking that I needed to get to the other side of this. It was scary to even think about stopping in the fog on a freeway. I didn't want to be a target for any rolling missiles back there.

A stop sign appeared in front of me. My hands jerked at the steering wheel. I heard a muffled screech of wet tires as I stood on the brake pedal, skidding out of control.

The signpost was going by in slow motion off to my right. I tried to watch it, but the shoulder belt had caught on my face, blocking my vision. I was tossed like a crash test dummy toward the passenger seat. I felt as though I were in a dream. Suddenly, everything stopped.

I pulled myself upright and looked around. There was a loud roaring in my ears. My heart pounded. My body shook uncontrollably. I fumbled with both hands to take the car out of gear.

I sat there a moment, just being still, trying to calm myself down, trying to figure out what had happened. How had I gotten off the interstate? Where had I ended up?

A few minutes passed before I finally reached over to the glove compartment and pulled out a flashlight. I pointed it down as I switched it on. I swung the car door open and climbed out onto the wet pavement.

For a long moment I stood leaning against the car door, trying to catch my breath. The oblong spot of light on the ground in front of me expanded and contracted with each gasp for air. I couldn't take enough air into my lungs. Finally, I forced in a deep breath, but it hardly satisfied my need.

I hurried to check around the car, making sure I hadn't hit anything. Through the fog, the side of the car was barely visible. I ran my hand along it, but found no damage.

Continuing on to the rear bumper there seemed to be a rough edge, a scratch, maybe. Had I clipped the stop sign? I walked back to take a look. The sign was standing, although it was bent back a little.

There were no street signs to tell me where I was or even the direction I had been going. I could tell only that I was at some kind of intersection.

I stood in the street, listening, waiting to hear another car, a cricket, or any other night sound. There was only dead silence. I thumbed the lock button on my keychain remote. The door locks clicked and the car horn sounded to inform me that all was secure.

I walked away from the car, still shaking and telling myself to be calm. I felt okay, not hurt at least. I brushed my fingertips gently along my right jaw line, where there was a burning sensation. It stung in the moist air and felt like the abrasions we used to get sliding into second base on those hard Central Valley ball fields growing up. We called it "getting a strawberry" because it would scrape off just enough skin to make it ooze red.

I pressed the sleeve of my sweatshirt against the strawberry, thinking it would stop the stinging. It didn't. I thought that walking in this direction would eventually lead me over or under the interstate. Instead, I walked into a bog. The heel of my left shoe sucked off, caught by the mud vacuum.

I plucked a fist-sized stone out of the muck and tossed it underhand ahead of me. There was the echoing "ker-plunk" that signified deep water. No point looking for a roadway in that direction. I supposed what I was looking for in my life wasn't going to be out there either.

Struggling blindly back toward the car, I would have walked right past it had I not smelled the odor of moist air on the hot exhaust and then turned to see the dimly-glowing interior light. The door was open. I remembered locking it. I pushed it closed.

I wanted to investigate the other side, but I was now afraid of getting lost out there in that fog. My stomach knotted. I still couldn't get enough air to breathe, and I couldn't stop shaking. I didn't like being alone out there.

I paused to think a moment and popped open the trunk. I was searching for something, anything, to help me establish a little certainty. There was a coil of rope and my backpack, packed with food and supplies.

In all the excitement, I'd forgotten about having packed them. I pulled them both out. Maybe I was stuck out in the middle of nowhere, but I wasn't going to go hungry—not that night—not yet.

Relaxing a little, I thought about my wife who had sent me out on this trip. A smile formed on my face as I remembered how she called me MacGyver, after a TV character she said could make a bomb out of a fountain pen and a bottle of rubbing alcohol. She thinks I'm always prepared for everything. I wished it were an episode of *MacGyver*. I'd yell, "Cut" and end the drama right then.

The rope's length was about 100 feet. I tied an end to the car bumper and walked up the roadway to the right, keeping the rope taut.

About forty feet out, I began stepping on large rocks. I treaded cautiously for a few more feet and then came up against a giant boulder. I tried to walk around it in both directions but found that it lay all the way across the roadway. Near the center was a small yellow sign that read "ROAD CLOSED."

Under the bottom of the yellow sign was a torn rectangle of cardboard with the words *Master Frogs Gorge* spray-painted in messy black letters across it and an arrow pointing to the left. I followed the rope back to the car.

Remembering my cell phone, I got into the car. Finally, I was able to take a full breath. It felt good. I paused a moment and took another and looked at my phone—no signal. Oh, well. I sat there breathing in deeply, holding it, exhaling, getting myself calm at last.

Suddenly, my mind raced again. This car has to get off the road. There'll be other cars. I started the engine and gunned the car across the intersection and over to the right edge of the road, pulling off as far as I dared, and stopped.

Outside again, I found the rope stretched back under the vehicle toward the intersection. I pulled it hand over hand until I clenched the end in my fist and began walking forward to investigate what lay ahead.

A few steps out I stopped and looked back; I pulled on the rope, making sure it was secure to the car. I thought about what it must be like for an astronaut on a space walk. I thought about home. I felt a sudden chill.

A bullfrog bellowed off in the distance. It seemed to be somewhere ahead of me. The presence of another creature, any creature, strangely comforted me in this solitary place. I remembered the cardboard sign—"Master Frogs Gorge."

Pausing again for a few seconds, I turned and went back to the car. I was done with exploring. I didn't need to end up in any gorge. I just wanted to get back on the freeway and out of that eerie place.

I started the car and slid the transmission into reverse, slowly pushing on the accelerator. I was mildly aware the car might already be stuck. It was.

Though my mind said it was time to panic, for some reason I stayed calm. My logic told me what steps to take: investigate the situation, get a clear idea of it, and then panic. Perhaps a course of action would manifest itself.

The rope was still tied to the bumper where I had coiled it, just in case. It turned out to be a good thing it was, because I did need to go out exploring again. I still didn't feel safe staying in the car. Who knew how bad the weather was going to turn, and what else might come down that road?

Folding down the rear seat to access the trunk, I pulled out a pair of old jogging shoes. Even in overwhelming circumstances, my mind wanted to protect my good shoes. It was something I had learned growing up, only getting new shoes once a year, at back-to-school time. I looked down at my feet and realized my left shoe was missing. I put the jogging shoes on, pulling the laces extra tight and rolling up my pant legs.

I stepped out and double-checked the knot on the bumper. I held tight to the rope, uncoiling it as I walked slowly away from the front of the car. The comfortable shoes were already soaked through, sticking and sloshing with each mud-caked step.

I trudged along, feeling top-heavy because of the backpack. Each step was a struggle to maintain my footing and hold the rope taut. The mud remained about the same depth over the distance. I thought I could feel a slight current flowing back toward the car.

For a moment, I thought, what if the car shifts and floats away. I dismissed that thought, partially because there was no excess tension on the rope, but mostly out of a need to believe in the rope as a lifeline. I tugged on it. The car was stable.

The bellowing frog, now getting louder, was the only sound I heard other than my own puffing and plodding. The grade had steepened noticeably. Again came that thought about the car slipping away. I tightened my grip on the rope.

I felt a burning pain in my palms and fingers from the friction of the rope. Why hadn't MacGyver packed a pair of gloves? There was about thirty feet of rope left.

I switched off the useless light to save the batteries. I knew I might need it later on. Fortunately, MacGyver had packed extras of those, and I was starting to think I might not find my way out of here soon. I was blind even with the light on, and I was beginning to get annoyed. I started to blame my wife for sending me out there.

Something solid bumped hard against the left side of my body. My arm extended automatically, feeling to the left, locating the immense boulder I had walked into.

The mud flowed beneath my feet. It now seemed to have changed direction from right to left, telling me its source was somewhere off to the right. The light still proved to be of no use. My scouting arm explored above my head. The rock was taller than I could reach.

I had a sense there was an opening to my right, but I still wanted to know how far the rock went to the left. As I felt my way around, it seemed it would go on forever. I started to think that I might run out of rope.

The rope. I didn't have hold of the rope. I must have dropped it when I bumped into the boulder.

Frantically working back to the right, I gripped the light with renewed urgency. Returning to the place where the mud had oozed beneath me, I groped on my hands and knees, desperately shining the impotent light all around. The rope was lost.

My heart seemed to stop and then started pounding again. Now it was time to panic. I had thoroughly investigated the situation, and the investigation had gotten me into an even worse situation than I had been in before.

I slapped my hand down hard at the ground, spattering mud everywhere. Why hadn't I tied that rope to my waist? The frogs stopped bellowing. All went silent.

I thought of trying to point myself back toward the car, but hesitated. Leaving this rock, I could wander around and end up in a hole or a deep bog.

My mind pictured one of those old movie scenes of a hat floating on a bed of quicksand. The next scene was of a dashing young policeman consoling my distraught wife as he handed my hat to her. The scene faded as I suddenly remembered that my good friend MacGyver had forgotten to bring my hat from the car.

Just as worse possibilities began to creep into my thoughts, a loud gushing sound crashed the silence. The air shifted. The suck of a sudden surge of mud rushed past me just to my right.

Whatever had been holding back the mud must have broken loose. There was a sound like a wall of mud avalanching down toward the car. Going back there now seemed pointless. The mud stopped gushing almost as quickly as it had begun.

I reached out with my foot and cautiously tested the ground for stability. The oozing mud had stopped. That was no real surprise. Whatever had been the source of it was depleted, for now.

I felt my way around the rock face, holding on where I could, stepping slowly and deliberately. I knew there was still danger, yet at the same time I was excited by the chance to explore the unknown. I was no longer tethered.

I felt the air change again and realized the situation had taken yet another turn. From where I stood, I could feel the rock face on the left. There was a gap in front of me, and another rock formation over to the right. The opening I sensed earlier was right there.

A breeze, ever so slight, blew against my face. I didn't want to go in, though it did seem a good place to gather my thoughts. I thought I might be able to see a little better in there as well. The moisture in the air outside was now annoyingly heavy. I was soaked through and cold.

Carefully stepping past the opening, I shifted my weight to one foot, grasping the rock face at the opening, feeling ahead of me with my hand and foot, thinking I would just follow along the rock to the right side and keep going as far as I could.

It took only a few seconds to find that the place where the mud had broken loose was right there. I stopped, shuddering with sudden fear. I turned around and went back to the opening. Shining the light inside, I entered.

CHAPTER 2

A Curious Awakening

"Wake up! Everyone wake up! We have a visitor!"

My eyes flew open and began darting back and forth as I lay there. My ears listened for any sound. Was that a dream, or did I really hear that? I did not remember any dream, only the words that jolted me awake.

I thought about my arrival the night before and raised my head up to look around. In the daylight, I could see that I was at the bottom of a deep gorge. The abrupt gray and black granite walls rose straight up behind the dense green foliage to a narrow crescent-shaped crack of blue sky. The strange and voluminous plants were intensely more dramatic than they had been in the field of my flashlight the night before. Some of the broad leaves were bigger than I was.

I was immediately overwhelmed by the indescribable floral multitude. A sheer waterfall plunged from so high I could barely see its source. The air teemed with drizzling mist, warm but not stifling. The overpowering beauty of the place was unlike anywhere I had ever seen before. My mind succumbed to the sensual treasures of this paradise to which I had awakened.

"Are you awake, sir?" I heard. "We did not wish to disturb your rest."

I propped myself up and looked around at ground level. To my astonishment, there were hundreds of frogs massed all around me, each with its gaze fixed right at me. My focus centered almost at once on a very large dark green frog with black and yellow specks and a yellowish underbody. It appeared to rise half a foot above the others. This big, fat frog was at least three times larger than any other frog I had ever seen.

Somehow, I sensed this gigantic frog was trying to communicate with me. Obviously, it couldn't speak. How could a frog speak? I rubbed my eyes and looked again.

"Yes," it said, as I looked into the blackness of its eyes. "I am communicating with you. Do not fear. I assure you that you will not be harmed and you may be glad of your visit with us."

I spoke aloud, more to myself than in reply, "Am I really awake? How can this be? Frogs don't speak. And, look at you, buddy. You're huge."

"Human. You are rambling and you are repeating yourself. I said I am communicating with you, not speaking. You are communicating with us all and you are speaking. Please do not speak, or only speak that which you wish to communicate. We do not require speaking here. It is not required anywhere, though you humans seem to think it is. We all have the ability to communicate, and that distracting noise you make only serves to distort your communication. I request that you just be with us and do not try to speak for now. You will communicate better that way. All your questions will be answered once you learn to be with us."

It certainly appeared this big frog really was communicating with me. The look on my face must have been one of utter disbelief.

I was startled by the wind, which suddenly blew a large leaf against the back of my shoulder. All at once, there was disturbed movement among the whole group of frogs. They all seemed to be startled at my being startled. I tried to relax, though my mind was flooded with many questions.

The big frog, who seemed to be the leader, communicated again.

"Human, we understand that you have questions. We will answer them for you if you will learn to be with us in a way that will allow you to understand us."

I heard myself respond without speaking, though I was really only thinking about my circumstances. "I don't know what you mean by be with…hey! I'm doing it! I'm communicating without speaking!"

My thoughts suddenly went out of control again, as I began to *think about* communicating rather than simply doing it. I tried to regain control, but my thoughts kept getting in the way.

"It is alright to have your thoughts, human. You can have your thoughts and not be with us. When you are able to be with us and not with yourself, you will communicate effectively. You just briefly experienced it. Be with us in a way that allows us to know what you are communicating."

"What is this place?" I asked.

My mind strayed again, and began evaluating how well I was doing. This time I was able to notice how I had been focusing on the frog when the communication worked, and how thinking about my thoughts had stopped producing the desired effect. I paused and looked at him.

"Very good, human," the big frog coached. "You will be communicating effectively before you know. You will learn much here and you will experience great enjoyment."

I shook my head and blinked in amazement. My eyes widened as I looked around at all the frogs. I was ready for some enjoyment. I kept looking into the big frog's eyes.

After a while, something started to become apparent that I hadn't noticed before. I had actually started to feel a kind of closeness with this big frog, almost like friendship.

Just as that began to occur to me, my thoughts again became jumbled and the feeling went away. I looked toward the waterfall, and then slowly around at the other frogs, actually pausing to notice many of them as individuals.

"Splendid, human!" The frog's voice sounded in my head.

I looked back at him and knew we really were communicating.

There was a lot of stumbling through at first, but I eventually began to get better at being with the big frog. He asked me to stop calling him the big frog. I laughed and asked him what I should call him. It was again time for me to learn something new.

My recollection of what the frog told me at that point is surprisingly clear, though I can't explain why. The more we communicated, the more it seemed to me that I was actually sharing his thoughts and not simply having a conversation. The frogs all moved in closer around me.

This is what Big Frog said:

> "You do not have to call me anything. You have known me, and there is no other who is me. When you relate to me as who I am and whom you know me to be, I will be who you know me to be, and no other. Do not try to understand this. Just continue to be with us and learn. It will go very quickly.
>
> "Human, for a long time I have known that you were special among humans. I have believed you could be the human who would bring people back into the real universe and carry the reflection from the light to the darkness. I believe it is your special purpose, though you shall not experience that during this visit. It is why the reflection remained here and why we allowed you to return here to our safe place.

"Few other humans have ever been here. This place exists in the human world only as distant possibility outside of conscious awareness. We travel extensively in your world because we have learned to understand it. Until now, no human has lived who could fully appreciate the possibility of our existence as we truly are and as you shall know us.

"In the world of humans, reality exists only in the language that humans speak with their tongues. The design of humans has been that everything must have a name assigned to it to have identity and be known. Frogs are called frogs by humans because they cannot exist without a name.

"Humans do not know about the world that exists outside of that which they can name. Humans know little of what there is to know, and they have almost no awareness of the possible existence of that which they do not know. This is not born of arrogance. It is by design. We have always viewed humans as an experiment.

"Although frogs had no part in creating humans, we considered that the Creator may have thought a certain economy could be obtained by creating a self-contained being—a being that did not require the Great Knowledge in order to exist in the world.

"The experiment was to give humans the ability to speak and create language. Language would then become the place where knowledge would be stored, thus freeing the human mind to experience a more true existence.

"It was well known by all creatures that humans had been given this ability and that the gift of language might someday be of use to us all. We watched and even participated insofar as we could."

At this point, I stood up abruptly and then sat down on the rock, looking directly at Big Frog. Something about the way the frog was being allowed me to understand his words. I was intrigued by everything he told me. The other frogs were frozen in place. Not even a breeze blew in the gorge.

"In the beginning, all creatures were able to communicate as we are now. Humans existed on the same level with us all. It was a great thing to watch as humans learned to use their new language ability, and it seemed indeed possible that more true knowledge could be attained in the freedom that language afforded.

"Nevertheless, humans eventually began to conceal some of their great achievements inside their language and began to use them to gain power over the universe. Though all creatures were able to communicate, even with the humans, the language caused duplicity to arise in the relationship.

"At first, it was in the humans' interest, because it served as a way to conceal their secret intentions from other creatures. They learned to control when they would communicate with the other creatures. They could receive our communication, but we were rarely able to receive theirs if they did not wish us to do so."

I shook my head, disbelieving the accusation that I was hearing from the frog. I thought about what I knew about the world and about my species. I looked around at the other frogs, sensing that I would be alone if I disagreed with what I was being told.

"Humans began to evolve rapidly, eventually eliminating competition from other creatures. They found ways to control us. They began gathering creatures and training them for labor. They slaughtered many creatures out of existence, often for sport.

"Human achievement began to come at the expense of other species. Over the millennia, humans dwelled in their secrecy and darkness until they had completely forgotten how to communicate in the old and true way.

"Humans believed themselves to be the Creator's chosen ones and thought they were superior to all others. They took the world as their own. Little remained of the oneness that life had been. Humans became separate as a species, and later as individuals.

"The world began to exist for them as something outside their bodies. They lost access to the Great Knowledge, and all that they knew existed inside of their language.

"They began to eat other living creatures, cultivating their arrogance into art as they learned to satisfy their particular tastes at a whim.

"Other creatures turned to darkness as a result of the human tragedy. Some began to take humans. Emulating the human way, they started eating the flesh of humans. This darkness turned against the creatures when, having lost their own integrity, they began eating other creatures as well. Even we frogs turned irreversibly to that path.

"A terrible evolution took place, and the world was changed from the great harmony that had been to a place filled with darkness and danger. Human beings sought to rule the world. Many creatures were eliminated from existence to make way for the great human emergence.

"We frogs gathered in Great Meetings to inquire into this phenomenon. The human experiment was declared failed. The future of life for us all began to get clouded in uncertainty."

I began to feel overwhelmed by the frog's testimony. Was he telling me that humans were to blame for animals becoming predators? I knew I had to be dreaming. I shook myself again, trying to wake up.

"It was viewed as fortunate that humans had forgotten how to communicate. Had they continued to use both communication and their exclusive language to gain power, all creatures might have been eradicated or evolved as slaves to the human endeavor.

"As it was, the frogs came to this place and some others like it on Earth. We cloaked our existence using the powers that humans had forgotten about. We live here as we always have and we remind ourselves of what life is and also about the possibility of possibility. We continue to gather periodically, bringing forth Great Meetings as we have for thousands of years since the humans made their most ominous decision.

"We have studied humans as part of this inquiry. We learned to penetrate the secrecy that humans created with their language. We have lived long among humans, sometimes suffering greatly for our trials. We have been studying and searching for the link that will allow us to bring humans back from the darkness.

"We never hated humans for who they became. It was not their fault that the language experiment gave rise to such destruction. They did not understand about their choices.

"Language was intended to improve us all. Knowledge exists as what we know. What we do not know exists as possibility. Experiments that are born of possibility and exist in possibility can take turns outside of predictability.

"None of the creatures, not even the humans, knew that the limitations of language might result in the loss of the communication that it was designed to serve. Though we all knew a world could be defined and exist within language, no one had conceived the possibility that communication could be cloaked under secrecy contained inside language. We were all very innocent then.

"The frogs are now ready to work with you as representative of human beings, not to restore the world as it was, but to create a new world in which all creatures are related and fulfilled. We invite you to the Great Meeting; but before that can happen, you must learn much and be thus prepared."

So it happened that I was invited to the Great Meeting of the Frogs. However, accepting their invitation was not as simple a matter as saying, "Yes, I'd love to be at your meeting."

First of all, I had to agree to learn more about how to conduct myself at the Great Meeting. There were training sessions for me to attend on communication and other technologies that I never knew existed. I was to learn how to operate in a way that would enable me to endure more than I ever thought possible.

The meeting was scheduled for twenty-three days after my arrival. I was told that the frogs were not holding this Great Meeting because of my arrival.

Great Meetings are held with each new moon and have been for thousands of years. The meetings are called an Inquiry into the Possibility of Being Alive.

I learned also that, even though I was an outsider and a human, the Great Meeting was not meant to be the frogs' meeting. The purpose of the meeting is to inquire into what is possible for all beings. I was to be as much a part of the Great Meeting as the frogs. Big Frog said I should not consider the Great Meeting to be like any meeting I had ever known.

Even though meetings take place each month, each one is a whole and complete process of discovery. Possibility is generated each time, not from the past, but from the future. These are the things I was to be coached on and taught in preparation for the Great Meeting.

Over time, I began to synchronize my speaking and my communication, such that my words became exactly what I intended to communicate. The longer I stayed with the frogs, the more effectively I communicated. I eventually found it natural to speak normally during my interactions, without being distracted by my internal thoughts. I also gained the ability to observe the frogs in their own authentic world, as they saw themselves.

CHAPTER 3

Getting Acquainted

Roaming freely through the secret bastion of the frogs that communicate, I was agape at the wondrous display of abundant nature wherever I looked. Frogs and toads of every species lived in this paradise. There were red, yellow, blue, brown, green, and even white frogs of every size, manner, and description.

I never saw even the slightest evidence of any strife or upset. I witnessed frogs doing things to one another that should have enraged them, yet not even as much as a single argument ever erupted.

I recalled the accident at the stop sign. I thought I remembered bumping my head on the way into the gorge. I wondered if I might have really been unconscious—if this was all just part of a comatose dream.

If it was a dream, I was reluctant to wake up. Something about these frogs demanded my being here with them, even if I were hallucinating the whole spectacle. Maybe my entire life had been nothing but a dream, but I wanted to learn, dream or not. I felt that something was available in this place. There was something I needed, something that I had come here to find.

I walked slowly through the thick grass, staying near the edge of the pond and creek. My eyes were drawn to any frog that showed up anywhere in the vicinity.

I began to study the frogs as they opened themselves up for my observations. Thinking about what Big Frog had said to me, I started a conversation with myself. Was the human emergence story a lie? Are humans the biggest cause of biological extinction since the dinosaurs died out?

These were serious charges levied against us by these frogs. If all this were true, what hope could there be for the future?

I recalled, in unfortunate graphic detail, the frog dissecting experiment from my high school biology class. I shuddered at the evil memory of it. I hoped the frogs would forgive me.

Suddenly, Big Frog sat before me.

"Oh, great," I thought. "I brought up the dissecting thing."

"Before progressing any further," he said, "you should take pause and consider what you may already think you know concerning the subject of frogs."

"Yes, I agree," I said, facing him with my hands clasped behind my back. "And it seems to me you are calling into suspicion the integrity of the whole human race."

I looked directly into Big Frog's eyes. I was now finding it easier to communicate by mouthing words silently, or even speaking them softly, as I formulated my communicative thoughts in my mind.

"In question is the integrity of all living creatures, not only human beings," he said. "Now, consider this. What if everything humans knew about frogs were nothing more than mankind's own conflated rendering of the truth as it evolved through the confined perspective that you yourselves placed on the world?"

I looked at the ground in front of my feet as I attempted to digest his words. I faced back at him and said, "I didn't understand you. What does that mean?"

"Mostly, if you tell the truth, humans do not think that the truth could possibly have anything at all to do with your perspective. It is the truth, after all. You know it is. You can prove it. That is why you call it the truth. Yet, what if you could consider, for even one moment, that what you know to be true about frogs might simply be your own explanation, your interpretation, of the phenomenon that you call frogs. What if it is not the truth, but a mere possible explanation? What if you simply inherited your ideas about frogs from ancestral observations, which over eons of societal proclamation have been interpreted and thus agreed upon as fact?

"Stories were handed down through your culture that perhaps arbitrarily decided that is the way frogs are. You studied frogs and took steps to prove what you already knew about them. You cut them open in your laboratories and analyzed their insides. You told new stories to validate your old stories about what you already knew in your minds to be true."

My concern about bringing up the high school dissecting experiment resurfaced. I suddenly had a mental glimpse of the definition I had placed on frogs.

Frogs: common name for amphibians that, along with toads, make up the order Anoura. Anourans inhabit all parts of the world except Antarctica, mostly preferring moist regions. Most Anourans begin life as eggs laid in water, hatching into tadpoles and later metamorphosing into adult frogs. Frogs are carnivorous, feeding principally on insects, spiders, worms, and other invertebrates. During hot or cold temperature extremes and in response to other ecological factors, many frogs are known to enter a state of torpor, or hibernation and estivation, in which the metabolic rate is depressed and many physiological functions are suspended for long periods of time. Frogs are sometimes used to control insects; as food; and also for laboratory and medical research due to the similarities of their skeletal, muscular, nervous, digestive, and other systems with those of higher animals.

Big Frog continued, "Mostly, you applied your own qualified human thinking to the observations you made on frog behaviors, which then became your truth. You believed it. It became your encyclopedia of frogs."

What Big Frog had said began to challenge the arrogance of my own thinking. Even as he spoke, I was making new assumptions based on my interpretations of what I had been seeing in this place.

It also seemed, to my amazement, that this frog was communicating using words I'd never heard before. This could not be a reflection of any dream from my own mind. Where could he have learned those words? What did they learn in those laboratories?

One of my observations over the last several days and nights was a seeming vanity among the frogs. Besides seeing that there were a few other extraordinarily large frogs among the group (I considered most of them to be more or less normal size), there seemed to be a cultural, if not a universal, attention they all paid to the appearance of their skin.

I learned, through my observations and by asking, that among a frog's most prized possessions is a tightly-stretched skin. They often go to great lengths to keep it that way, sometimes spending hours in a particular muddy area moistening their skin, soaking up nutrients, and then climbing onto a warm rock to dry in the sun.

Another observation was that the frogs seemed to always have a question on their minds, though it did not seem quite so pressing that they ever sought any answers. Moreover, they seemed to never allow anything to bother them. There was a characteristic matter-of-factness about them, a kind of a formality in the way they always conducted themselves with each other, and even with me. It was as if they found it greatly important to demonstrate respect for all.

I took the words of Big Frog into account and continued exploring, venturing farther away from the water and toward the steep rock walls.

Walking among the frogs and seeing them around me, I began to have a humorous thought. It seemed as though I had heard it spoken to me, though I couldn't say it was any frog that had said it. I thought it must have come out of my own mind.

The phrase, "Though it was in their nature to be, not one of them dressed the part," was a curious one that I couldn't begin to explain. The first time I had heard it was while I had been thinking about the almost formal appearance of the frogs.

I had no idea why that particular thought played in my mind. It had no particular meaning for me. Frogs do, in fact, all dress the same, which is not at all, and being is their nature.

Somehow, though, it seemed they all received my strange thought as humorous, and I sensed they were pleased with it. Maybe they understood why it had occurred to me.

Around that same time, I had begun to notice a particular little frog showing up in different places around the gorge. Not only had it appeared practically everywhere I went, the thing often seemed to be situated very strangely in many of the places where it appeared. It was as though it had been frozen each time in the act of moving, or was maybe even posing for my benefit.

The strange frog kept moving around mysteriously from place to place, and I began to think it was toying with me. One time, I saw it sandwiched between a broad leaf and a rock. I looked away for just a moment, and when I looked back, the frog was curiously all the way on the other side of the pond.

I tried many times to catch that strange frog in the act of moving, but it seemed too clever for me. Once, I even created a game out of my attempt to trap it. It was a game for me, if not for the strange little frog.

There was yet another odd thing about that frog. It was something about its appearance. The thing seemed to defy the way frogs were supposed to look.

For one thing, its skin hung loosely on its body. Its legs were short and stubby. Its body was ill-formed and less frog-like. I could tell it was some kind of a frog, but it was very different from all the others.

Having some basic understanding of the general way frogs are supposed to be, one of my most ardent pursuits became the study of this one frog. It never moved when I was watching it. Sometimes it sat inanimate for very long periods of time. I was never sure it saw me, though my sense was that it did.

I tried repeatedly, and always unsuccessfully, to communicate with it the way I had been talking with the other frogs. I eventually began to call into question my own ability to communicate. It was as though all I had learned about communicating had now been lost for some reason.

I continued to correspond with the others, though none of them would ever let me in on why that one particular frog wouldn't respond to me. They just behaved as they normally did, as though everything was exactly the way it was supposed to be.

Still, I kept coming back to that one strange little frog, hoping to reach a breakthrough. What was it about that particular frog? Why was it suddenly so important to me?

There had to be something about that frog. I couldn't figure out what it was. Maybe it was the challenge of communicating with it, but I didn't think that was it. It seemed like communication was exactly what was happening. I simply didn't understand its language. Certainly, some interaction was occurring between us.

One thing seemed clear. This frog had been following me around for the last several days, if not from the very beginning. My mind came up with myriad explanations for its existence, some of which no doubt amused the other frogs. They never revealed their judgments to me though. If, in fact, they had been judging me, they never once reacted to my judging them, which did occur a lot.

I started to question who the frogs thought they were, having a weird frog follow me around like some secret agent. It wasn't even good at sneaking. I saw it every time, and certainly knew when it was around, playing its little game. Still, I never saw it move. It was very clever about that.

Once, I even tried to trap the strange creature into moving. I looked at it very deliberately, and then looked away and back again very quickly several times. Of course, there it was, each time, always right in the exact spot where it had been.

Finally, one time there was an exception. Just as I was giving up the game, I looked away, and when I looked back, the strange little frog was gone. It had disappeared from the spot and was nowhere to be found.

I looked jubilantly up at the sky, thinking, "Yes, I have caught it this time." Then, looking back at the original spot, there was that frog, as though it had always been there. It was a very strange little frog.

When I couldn't take it any more, I made the decision to stare it down. I was going to catch it moving or else.

I pulled down a pair of spongy leaves from a plant the frogs had shown me. These leaves had an exquisite sweet taste and were very satisfying to the appetite. Situating myself with the water within easy reach, and without taking my eyes off the frog, I determined to see the frog move even if it meant staying there all night.

I sat myself in a comfortable position and the stare-down began. The frog looked unaffected and didn't seem to care at all about my rude staring. I stared on. The frog did not move.

After a period of time, which seemed pretty long to me and may well have been not too long, I caught myself drifting into wayward thought. My attention wavered as imaginings began to enter into my mind, but I had caught myself before they damaged my prospects. I resolved to be more purposeful about the whole project.

I kept the stare going, at least for a little longer. A while later, the drifting thoughts came back. I almost looked away, but caught myself again.

I became irritated about that and thought I should try something else. I decided to reach out and touch the frog. I thought, in my arrogance, maybe it would understand that I only wanted to communicate with it and it would finally initiate a dialogue with me.

Reaching out, my hand was nearly there. I could feel energy from the frog in my fingertips. I was just about to touch it. Then I blinked. I couldn't avoid it. It just happened.

When my eyes reopened an instant later, the frog was gone again. I was enraged. I started cursing loudly.

All the frogs cleared a wide space to avoid me. Some plopped into the water, while others jumped or climbed away into the rocks.

I picked up a palm-sized river stone and hoisted it above my head as if to smash it down in anger. Suddenly, I heard a familiar voice in my head.

"Stop now. Do not drop that stone," the voice of Big Frog commanded.

The sense I had was that compliance was mandatory and wise, though at the time I really didn't want to listen. I calmly lowered the rock, laying it gently down on the ground.

I said back to Big Frog, "I'm sorry. I wasn't going to hit any frogs with it. I was just going to smash it onto the ground. I've been getting really frustrated by my failure to communicate with that other frog."

"To which other frog do you refer?" Big Frog asked. "Is one here that I am not acquainted with?"

CHAPTER 4

Night Journey

Late that evening I sat amidst the frogs and recounted the strange journey that had brought me into the gorge—the drive along the interstate, that crazy fog, the stop sign, the accident, the terror of being alone and lost.

The frogs seemed more interested in my experience entering the passageway into the gorge than the rest of it. I began to think that most of them had never gone through that passage themselves.

It was during this conversation that I began to realize that these frogs were not mind readers. For them to know my experience of the passage, I actually needed to intend to communicate it to them, which was only slightly more complicated than simply thinking about it to myself.

I still wasn't sure if that was true for Big Frog. He and a few others, I would find out later, seemed to have powers above those of the normal frog population. They seemed to know a great deal about my thoughts and feelings all the time.

I began describing my avoidance of the rock crevice and how I had finally decided to enter.

❈   ❈   ❈

Once inside, I began to feel secure and warm. I sat down on a small rock to rest. The fog hadn't penetrated the opening. Pointing the light upward, I saw that I had entered a large crevice between two immense rock formations. I sensed there was an opening above, but the top of the crack curved away to the right.

Ahead of me, the light seemed to diffuse into darkness before reaching the other end. The width of the crevice appeared consistent. The floor was relatively flat.

The view was hazy looking back toward the opening. I was no longer interested in going back that way.

After a short rest I decided to go on, glancing once more in the direction of the opening. Maybe I was still interested after all. I knew the car was back there somewhere.

In the interest of conserving batteries, I turned the light off and felt my way along. I considered myself lucky to have a good light with new batteries. I expected they would last a couple of hours with conservative use before I'd have to put in the extras.

Every now and then, I illuminated the area ahead just to be sure nothing obstructed the way and to see if there was an end to the crevice—nothing, and not yet.

I had gone far enough that the rock where I had rested was barely visible looking back. There was still no change in the forward direction. I walked on.

A few minutes farther along I shined the light ahead. I noticed a reflection. There was nothing recognizable. I could just see that something was different. I turned the light off again and moved a little faster now.

I started thinking I should not get too excited. I still needed to be careful. I slowed a bit.

Another few minutes along, I shined the light ahead again. This time I could definitely tell something was there. I could distinguish a color, green. It was not yet possible to determine the size of the shapeless green something. I still had no depth perception. I kept moving.

After fifty to sixty more steps with no perceptible change in the green reflection, I switched off the light and slowed my pace again. I dragged myself along, now beginning to feel the tiredness in my body, thinking about my car, thinking about my wife, and thinking about my own mortality.

I didn't really sense danger in that moment, but a worry for the future had started to come over me. For some reason, I knew I needed to get through this passage, regardless of whatever might be on the other side.

I stopped again to rest and pointed the light toward the mysterious green color. Something new was there. There was a shape, a smooth texture, like a surface of something.

I started toward it almost at a run, keeping the light fixed directly at the object. I felt a thud. Everything went dark—spinning. There was intense pain in my forehead. I stumbled, then caught myself. I went down on one knee.

Moments passed. My senses began to return. My forehead throbbed with a dull ache and a sharp pain right in the center.

The light was on the ground, still shining but much dimmer. I could make out the jutting rock where I had smacked my head in that foolish rush. I touched my fingers to my forehead expecting to find a gash but there was no blood. It had been a solid hit, just knocking me senseless. I deserved it.

A slight swelling was already noticeable by touch just below my hairline. How stupid I had been to run in there. It was so dark. I would not do that again.

I instinctively tapped the light to get it going, however, the filament must have broken when I dropped it. Now I really was in the dark.

Amazingly, I didn't panic about the light. I had been groping for so long I was actually pretty used to it. Anyway, it seemed that having the light on was how I had gotten myself into the worst trouble.

I began feeling my way along again. My head throbbed. I resolved to be more careful this time. I realized I'd left the backpack at the place where I had fallen. I needed to go back for it.

I switched on the flashlight with no bulb and calmly walked back to the exact spot, reaching down in the dark, pointing the inoperative light as if actually illuminating the area. I picked up the pack by the strap and tiredly hefted it up to my shoulder, letting it dangle as I shifted my upper body forward, over-compensating for the medium weight of the pack.

I started out again following the darkened beam of the defunct flashlight, with no lingering thoughts of the jutting rock.

I was not sure at first, but it seemed I could make out just a bit of that green shape even in the darkness. Maybe there was another opening close by. Something brushed gently against the side of my face and tapped against the back of my head.

A slight breeze started to blow warm air, much warmer than where I had come from. I could smell something, but I couldn't determine what it was. It seemed there was a bit of moisture in the air, but not like on the other side of the opening.

What had brushed against me were the leaves of a large plant, maybe a tree. I felt its thick stems. I didn't want to reach out too far. I was tentative, not knowing what other creatures could be lurking in this dark place.

I again became aware of the darkness and wished for the light to work. Standing still, keeping my breath as quiet as possible, I listened as I shivered with new fear.

A moment later, I had a thought, that MacGyver might have packed a spare bulb for his flashlight. I fumbled for the end of the flashlight cylinder, unscrewing the metal cap and feeling inside. There was a bulb. MacGyver had come through after all. What a guy. I hoped the bulb would work.

I heard something move not far away from me—*slide, shuffle, stop, slide, shuffle, stop*. I was suddenly aware that I had been hearing that bellowing again, now very close by. Maybe it had never stopped. Was it really a bullfrog?

I quickly took out the damaged bulb, put the new one in, and turned it on. There was light. Color leaped out at me from the beam.

The plant I had brushed against loomed huge before me. There were many more all around, with gigantic flowers of white and orange and red. I thought I recognized the sweet smell of plumeria blossoms, but none of the plants looked at all familiar to me. This grotto reminded me of a tropical jungle—but in Arizona?

I swept the light from side to side. All around me were tropical-looking plants. I caught sight of a waterfall and then noticed I had been hearing the roar of falling water. Sounds began to jump out from everywhere—water, rustling leaves, croaking frogs. Just ten feet from me was a pool that looked deep and dark.

I had a sense of being in a giant hole, maybe inside a mountain. The walls near me were sheer, rising farther than the light would reflect. I was excited.

I couldn't wait for daylight to see it all. My fear disappeared. Everything was so beautiful. Then I heard that sliding-shuffling sound again. I was not alone. The fear came back.

I quickly started shining the light in all directions along the ground. I heard a slapping sound, followed by a plunk in the water. Plunking sounds began to echo all around me. I saw glimpses of dark creatures landing at the surface of the pool and disappearing into it.

I remembered the bellowing bullfrogs. It must be them. It seemed there were a lot of them around, and why not? They probably had no one to disturb them in here. Maybe even no natural predators. I hoped there were no predators, natural or otherwise.

Standing there, a strange sense of calm began to wash over me. A few minutes later, the calm was replaced by exhaustion.

I found a reasonably dry spot on a nearby flat rock. I sat down and leaned against a tree. Pulling down a few broad leaves, I rolled them up in the hood of my wet sweatshirt and lay back on the rock. I felt surprisingly comfortable.

A narrow curve of dark sky was visible above, scattered with stars in unfamiliar constellations. For a brief moment, I wished I had learned more about the stars. Was that the Big Dipper there, upside down? Maybe not.

The frogs began coming back out of the water, making wet slapping sounds with their pads as they hopped. Their fat bodies plopped against the rocks. I could tell they were close by, and I was comforted by their presence. Something about them being there made me feel safe.

Even that night, before meeting the frogs, as I lay there falling asleep, I somehow knew I was supposed to be in this place. Something had drawn me here. Maybe this was the adventure I was supposed to have. Maybe I was going to find what I was looking for in these mountains.

CHAPTER 5

Word and Integrity

My eyes cracked open to a lazy overcast morning. I lay in that nebulous state somewhere between lucidity and the last vestige of sleep that wants to keep hold of me. A new voice sounded, calling out to me. It was a childlike voice.

Finally roused to full wakefulness, I looked around. This was my first notice of any other than adult frogs in this place. It was something I had been wondering about. Where are the children?

The voice sounded again, in that begging tone a child will often use, "Please play with me. There is no one to have fun with."

I stood very still. All my senses engaged to locate the source of this new voice. There were no frogs in sight.

"Please play with me."

There it was again, but I couldn't find it.

Beginning to wonder if this might be a voice out of my own mind, I thought it could be a kind of a reaction to my isolation here. "No," I thought in an internal voice that sounded like my own. "It's not me."

"No," the child said. "I am here. Come play with me now." The request had turned into a demand.

Even with my recent experience learning to communicate with the frogs, I still thought this might be a trick. Instinct told me something was off. I should be wary. It didn't seem normal even for here. My eyes searched suspiciously for the source of the ruse.

The sun broke through the clouds just in time to aid me in the search. As I gazed out over the pond, my attention latched onto something moving in the sun-illuminated water near me. Minuscule, and a surprise to me that I had seen it at all, there was a tadpole, a pollywog.

I heard the voice again. "Yes, play with me."

My mind didn't believe such powerful communicative energy could come from such a speck of a creature as this tiny precursor to a frog. The bratty little tadpole wanted me to play.

Amazed, maybe even more than in my first morning here, I was now communicating with an infant frog. I extended my hand gently into the pond, where the pollywog immediately started playing tag with my finger, flirtatiously nudging and darting off before I could touch it back.

I began to play with the tadpole, feigning disinterest and then aggressively trying to catch it. The future frog was too fast and playful. It knew my movements before I even twitched. We were both having fun.

I began to chase the little one around the pond in a fit of laughter. All at once, I found myself playing tag with dozens of tiny pollywogs, all darting up at my fingers and then swimming away as soon as I thought about trying to catch one of them. Time and purpose became lost in the wake of the game.

"Human…" I suddenly recognized Big Frog's voice. "You have no integrity. We thought you could be with us, yet you demonstrate otherwise."

"What do you mean?" I said, suddenly afraid of the powerful frog. "I don't know—"

"You made a promise, yet you do not keep it," the great frog interrupted. "You cannot be trusted. You have no relationship to your word. You are not who we thought you were. Who are you? Why are you here?" The frog made no sense.

"I don't understand. Why are you saying these things?" I was indignant. My fear was inexplicable. I had no idea who these frogs thought I was.

"What are you talking about?" I asked. "I made a promise? I have no relationship to my word?"

"You have no integrity and you do not even know it," Big Frog said.

I was hurt by its accusations.

"Who are you?" the frog repeated.

"Are you asking me my name now? I don't understand. You said names are not required. You already know who I am." I was confused and defensive. "Didn't you say that speaking words interrupts communication? Why do you want to talk about my relationship with words?"

The frog didn't answer my questions. It continued with what I perceived as riddles.

"Word is not speaking," he said, "as language is not communication; neither is speaking being your word. You speak your thoughts as you spit out your language. You translate communication into your language and interpret with your thoughts. Your thoughts neither serve you nor do they serve the universe. You have no relationship with who you are and you do not know it. Answer this now. Who are you that you are?"

I couldn't understand anything the frog was saying to me. I have no relationship to who I am. I supposed the frog was right about that, and I was either now being rejected as a failure or I was learning a new lesson. My instinct was to think I was being rejected.

"Okay, fine!" I said. "So I don't know what I'm talking about. I don't know what you're talking about. You think I'm supposed to just take this all in. One minute I'm driving my car and the next I'm here in this place having my world turned upside down? I'm just supposed to give up everything I've ever known about the world and believe that I'm not dreaming this right now?"

"We have no expectation that you shall ever wake up from the dream that is your life," the frog responded. "The illusion you humans call the world is indeed a powerful one. All but a few of you are caught up in your unyielding view that the world is as your senses tell you and as you believe it to be. In that illusion, there is no choice but to be the illusion. It is a world of separation and individuality. You strive to become that which you already know yourselves not to be.

"Since the experiment began, eons ago, a handful of informed humans have spoken bits of the truth. Humans named these people as prophets, yet those who came after them always perverted the messages they brought.

"Truth has been covered over by the illusion wrought of human thinking, the illusion of time and of cause and effect. Through the invention of these, humans have lost the notion that all is possibility and that possibility manifests through word. As all is possibility, so is possibility related to word. I ask you: who are you that you are and that the world is?"

"I don't understand your question," I replied. "Who am I that I am and that the world is? I don't know."

Anger began to well up within me.

"That you do not know, human, is the result of your thoughts. Your thoughts cannot know who you are. There is no possibility for knowing who you are. Who you are is who you are and your opinion about that has no bearing on the matter.

"Your opinions about yourself serve only to conceal who you are from yourself. You identify yourself with your thoughts and then you think—you opine—that who you are is who your thoughts have identified you as being."

The frog paused as if to gauge my ability to understand and stay in the conversation.

I started to realize that the frog was engaging me in a powerful inquiry. I had a sense of something quite momentous beginning to happen.

My body started to feel heavy and lethargic. My breathing became labored. I felt dread fear and at the same time great excitement. They were the same conflicted feelings as when I had lost the rope and entered the dark passage that brought me into this world.

During this interlude, I began to recall a time in my childhood when I was about four years old. My parents had taken the whole family to the annual county fair. It wasn't my first time at the fair, but it was an eventful day that will always stand out in my memory.

The fairgrounds were located along a six-lane divided highway, two or three blocks down and across from the old County Hospital. My father parked our brown and white Chevy station wagon in the hospital parking lot. We were in the next-to-last row facing away from the highway.

Three of my brothers, one of my sisters, and I piled out of the car along with my parents. We joined my grandparents, with my older brother and sister, parked nearby.

We all walked down to the fairgrounds together. My mother held onto my hand as we crossed the heavily traveled highway at the traffic signal.

All was well inside the fair. As always, I avoided the fast rides, particularly the ones that went high up into the air.

Staying close to my mom, I looked around suspiciously at the carnival people. Even at that young age, I had already formed an opinion that they were different from normal people, like us. Something about them excited me, but I feared their strangeness.

Out of the corner of my eye, I saw something interesting on display at one end of a booth where my mother and I had stopped. I wanted to get closer to look at it.

Pulling at Mom's hand, I urged her to come my way, but she had found something interesting herself and wouldn't budge. My hand pulled free from hers as I was drawn over to look at the commanding object. My memory of what it was has long since faded.

Having fulfilled my curiosity, or maybe just wanting her to buy the thing for me, I turned expectantly toward Mom. She was not there.

I panicked and immediately started running all over, looking for her. She was nowhere to be found. In fact, not one member of my entire family was anywhere to be seen.

I started running wildly back to all of the places I remembered seeing anyone in my family. It seemed as though every one of them had just vanished.

I stopped and stood still, drawing my arms in, with one fist clenched inside the other, and pulled tightly against my chest, my chin touching my hands. I became frightfully aware that I was now alone in a sea of strangers—and they were all carnival people.

My training had always been, "NEVER TALK TO STRANGERS." I looked around at the strange people and concentrated on appearing calm on the outside, not wanting to draw any attention to myself.

I passed by the police booth, only briefly considering talking to those strangers. However, my natural assertiveness took over, and I thought, "I can take care of this myself. I'll find them."

I walked quickly toward the front gate under the assumption that if they all had left without me, I might catch them before they got to the car. Why did they leave me?

I looked at the tall metal revolving gate consisting of a rotating vertical pole with rows of horizontal bars that meshed with a column of stationary bars. Its design allowed only one person at a time to exit and at the same time prevented anyone from entering from the outside.

There was a gate like that at the zoo. My brothers and I had spent plenty of fun time trying to fool that one, but now I had to manage pushing those heavy bars by myself without attracting the attention of any strangers.

With the help of an elderly woman who apparently was not a carnival person and thought my parents were already outside, I made it out.

I ran like the wind down the street to the traffic signal. Out of breath and pressing the heel of my hand against the sharp pain in my side, I saw the car across the street. No one was there.

My mind was still racing. Maybe they walked another way and I just missed them. I pushed the button for the "walk" signal and calmly crossed the street.

In the late nineteen-fifties people left their cars unlocked in our town. No one thought much about dishonest people in those days, and nobody would want our old station wagon anyway.

I opened the back door and scrambled onto the hot seat. I was suddenly afraid and immediately locked all the doors. There were strangers around.

I thought about a conversation I was not supposed to have heard between Mom and my oldest brother. They'd been talking about a suspicious man in our neighborhood who had been seen posing as a policeman.

Mom had speculated that the man might be trying to take children. I had asked her why he would do that.

"Never you mind about that," she told me. "You just stay away from strangers, young man."

I promised.

Not wanting anyone to see me from outside the car, I lay myself down across the seat. It was a hot fall day and the vinyl car seat burned against the side of my face. I placed my tiny palm against the seat and lay my face on the back of my hand.

I started to cry. With my jerky breaths reaching only the tops of my lungs, I fell asleep there in the heat of our sun-drenched car.

Nearly an hour passed. There was a knock on the window. I jumped in disoriented fear that quickly gave way to disoriented elation as I saw my older brother Charlie. He was the second oldest of the boys.

I quickly unlocked the door and pulled at the handle, hearing the distant sound of Charlie's voice.

"We thought you might be here," he said.

Back inside the fair, I hugged my mom tight. For the rest of the day I was treated like a most special person. Everybody felt sympathy for the little boy who had been lost.

"And he was so smart…he went right to the car and waited." My mom told the story forever. "We should have known that was where he'd be. He's so smart."

I knew right then that for me to be special, I'd have to always be smarter than everyone else.

Why did I recall this episode during my inquiry with Big Frog? I had the same feeling in my body that I had felt that day when I was lost at the fair. It was the fear of being lost in the unknown.

"Very good, human," the frog said. "You are present. We can have this dialogue now."

I wasn't sure I would have said I was present. My first thought was to ask if we had not already been having a dialogue, but I realized the frog had been attempting to communicate with me while I was engaged in a monologue with my own thoughts about what he was saying.

I now had a sense of being engaged, and I was ready for the lesson. At the same time, I knew I didn't want to be having this conversation at all. It was as though my mind was afraid I might not be able to survive as intense a dialogue as this one promised to be.

"Okay," I said to the frog. "I am in this conversation, but I want you to know I don't think I am going to enjoy it."

"It is wise to have that awareness, yet it shows great courage for you to stand and engage in a conversation that could well prove fatal to the identity you have attached to yourself," the frog answered.

"Funny, I was just thinking of the word suicide," I remarked, still not totally convinced this was a healthy conversation for me. "I'm sure that I'm not anywhere near where I need to be to grasp this whole concept."

"You may be right about that," Big Frog said. "However, it may also be that you are in the perfect place to have this conversation. If you were not, your mind would have already taken you away. Perhaps there is no right place for you to be in for this inquiry to happen. You may never be ready, but I assure you that you are indeed prepared."

"Okay, then let's look at this business about who I am that I am," I said. "It seems to me there is something I am resisting about that. If I could just set whatever that is aside, I think I could at least begin to understand the question you're asking me."

"Very good!" The frog seemed joyous. "Keep going."

"All right," I continued. "So, I'm looking at what that resistance might be, but I don't yet see what it is. I really feel like just running away and not...or somehow...just avoiding the whole thing."

"Yes," the frog said. "The identity that you believe yourself to be shall defend itself. You will experience all that the survival instinct can manifest. It could be said that human identity lives and breathes inside of your thoughts. Identity was invented by humans, but it was born of the great experiment. It is of you. Whatever you create, you become the effect of it."

"Now, that is something that I think we'll have to look at later. I want to nail this 'who I am that I am' thing," I said, miming quotation marks in a gesture that was sure to baffle the frog.

Big Frog made no remark about the gesture, but conceded, "That will be okay for now. And, you may see that it is very much a part of it."

"Fair enough," I said. "Now, you said something about my thinking not serving me. It seems to me I should look at that first to see how it relates to your question."

I continued, "So, if thinking my thoughts will not give me an answer, then I might need to look at something that is not part of my normal thinking, but which can somehow move me toward a conclusion or realization." I paused, thinking for a moment. "I find it all just perplexing," I said.

"Yes," the frog said. He had been sitting quietly, yet his presence overwhelmed me. "And consider that an answer is precisely what your thinking is going to give you. Answers are what your mind seeks in order to move you toward any conclusion or realization."

"Okay, I can accept that for now. And I see that this has something to do with communication and that whole business of having a relationship to my word," I said. "So, if it's about communication, but it's not the thoughts, what is the difference between my thoughts and communication?"

I was trying to get my head around the idea. "It seems like thoughts are communication, if only inside my own head. Oh, wait! I think I do see something! Thoughts are communication, but only with myself. When I communicate with only myself, I have only my own mind to draw any conclusions from. When I am communicating with someone else, as in a dialogue with you, I have access to something other than what I already know, or think I know."

"You are getting there," the frog said. "Just keep looking and asking yourself who you are being. Who are you that you are?"

"Who I am that I am is…" I stopped. "I still don't get it. Who I am that I am…I can't see. So, let me try it this way. If who I am is who I say I am, then who I say I am is…who?"

"Precisely," the frog said, as though he now thought I knew something.

I stood there looking at him with a blank expression. "Okay, now," I said. "If who I am is who I say I am, then that would mean I actually do have a say in the matter, right?" I was looking to the frog for his approval.

"You have always had a say in the matter. Who you are has always been who you say you are, not necessarily who your mind thinks you are. It has always been so, and so it shall always be." More riddles from the big frog.

I looked at him blankly again. "Wait a minute, something might be happening over here. I don't know what, but something. I just saw…"

I paused again and looked into the frog's eyes. "I think…what I can see is that I am who I say I am, which is to say, not a product of my thoughts. But, if that's so, then I'm not sure how I can say who I am in a way that will actually mean anything."

"Go on," the frog urged.

"Well, I don't know who to say I am other than whom my thoughts tell me about who I am or who I wish to be. It seems like I'm looking for the right way to say it, and it seems like that has to come from my thoughts."

"Look again at what I said to you earlier," the frog said. "I said you have no relationship to your word, and you have always had a say in the matter."

"I know that's a clue but...I don't know," I said, confused. "So, I have no relationship to who I am...what does that mean? Maybe it means I don't know what I'm saying. Maybe I don't understand, or...I don't understand the impact of what I say."

Something clicked. "Yes, I have always said and I've never understood that which I say...wait! I think I have it! Maybe what I say about myself does create who I am, and having no relationship to my word, I am always blindly creating who I am without having the slightest awareness of what I'm creating."

It was becoming clearer. "Whatever I create, I become the effect of it. So, I create what is in my thoughts and then become the effect of my thoughts. I become my thoughts or—aha! Who I am that I am is who I think I am in my thoughts. That's the answer to your question. I am that my thoughts are who I am rather than being who I say I am or who I really am. And, being the effect of my thoughts just keeps me stuck in my thoughts. I created my own identity out of my thoughts and then became the effect of the identity I created. I don't have an identity—my identity has me."

"Who are you that you are?" Big Frog pressed.

"I am that I am...who...I am that I am...that's it! I am that I am, and that's all. Who I am is that I am!" My body suddenly felt light, as though a weight had just been lifted off me. My lungs felt as though they had expanded beyond my ability to take in enough air to fill them. "Suddenly, I can see...what...I can see is...possibility?"

"Yes," the frog said. "Very good."

"Wow!" Excitement engulfed me. I felt tingling energy all over my body. After a long, silent pause, I remembered that the lesson wasn't over yet.

I addressed Big Frog again. "Now, about the promise I didn't keep. Let's talk about that. I'm ready to clear this whole thing up."

"Okay."

"I wasn't clear about the promise that I did not keep and I want to be clear about that."

I was now the one issuing a challenge.

"Did you not agree to be trained and prepared for the Great Meeting?" Big Frog asked.

"Well, yes, I did agree, and—"

"We are having this dialogue now because you did not keep your promise," the frog explained. "This is a simple matter. Do you not understand that you were not being your word?"

"I…uh…well…" I thought about how the morning had begun. "Okay, I see that I was not really engaged in my training. The little ones lured me to the pond."

"Ah, so you were lured away from your promise by children?" The question stung like an angry wasp. "Not unlike, I suppose, that time at the fair when you so willingly let go of your mother's hand to pursue the whim of a child."

"Yes, I did allow myself to be lured away. I guess I wasn't thinking about training at that time. I didn't think I was supposed to be training at that moment. I'm used to just getting up each morning and exploring until I find myself engaged in a lesson. I know of no agreed upon time," I explained.

"So, you are saying that you are not on any particular training schedule and thus you did not need to be your word to be trained?" the frog asked, but it seemed more like a statement to me.

"Well, the part about the training schedule is right—I don't know about the rest," I said defensively.

"So, at the moment you made your promise to be trained, were you being trained?" the unrelenting frog asked.

"Well, I am now," I responded.

"Yes, I think you are," the frog said. "And, what do you think is possible regarding the training that you are receiving now?"

"I can see," I began, "that I always, every minute, have a choice and an opportunity to be who I say I am. And that when I allowed myself to be lured away, I was making myself unavailable for training. I was not being my word."

"So," the frog said, "what do you mean that you 'were not being your word?'"

"Well, I meant that…I meant that I can be lured away from my promise," I answered, as I was beginning to appreciate the insight.

"Yes, you *can* be lured away," the frog agreed. "And, what does it mean that you can be lured away?"

"I was afraid you were going to ask that," I said, still trying to get to an answer from my thoughts. "It means that I don't always think about keeping my word...I give in to whims and I can't be relied upon to do what I say."

"Is that bad?" the frog asked.

"Well, it seems like it is. I never really thought about how much it gets in the way of accomplishing what I want in my life. Now, I can see how it happens everywhere in my life. It's true that I allowed myself to be lured away from my mother at the fair."

I suddenly thought about my mother. I thought about how much I always loved her. Pausing, I gathered myself. "I see now how that was a case of me being lured away from the promise I made to stay close to her. And that has happened many times in my life. I say I will do something, and then I find all kinds of other pursuits to keep me from doing it. I get distracted too easily."

I was seeing a major trend in my life unfold.

"Is that bad?" Big Frog asked again.

"Yes, I think so. It has cost me a lot more than I have been willing to admit. I could be much more effective in many areas of my life if I were not so easily distracted," I said remorsefully.

"And what if I said that is neither good nor bad...that it is part of your humanity?" the frog asked. I again sensed I was being led somewhere.

"Yes, and my considering it as bad is something I do in my own thoughts." I added. "That's just another way of being distracted, isn't it? Another way of not owning up to what I say. I make up my mind that it's bad and it becomes about me. Then it turns into a story that I am bad. This is a very nasty business, isn't it?"

"It can certainly look that way," the frog said. "And what does it mean if you see you are not being your word?"

"I suppose it doesn't really mean anything," I responded. "I am who I say I am."

"And there are consequences regarding how you relate to your word," Big Frog said. "So I ask you, are you your word?"

"Yes, I am my word," I said proudly.

"Yes, when you are being your word—and being a human there will be times when you are not," the frog warned.

"So, you are saying I can't be my word all the time?" I asked.

"I am not saying you cannot be your word all the time. However, if you expect that you will always be your word, you will be disappointed when you are not. Disappointment lives in your thoughts and interpretations. Your thoughts do not give you access to all of what is possible. As soon as you impose your expectant thoughts on any outcome, you become the effect of your intention rather than the possibility of what you spoke."

"Okay," I said. "I think I have it. I'm sure that I'm making it more complicated than it really is. I am being my word when I am being my word. Whenever I think I have to be my word I am actually only thinking about being my word, and not being it."

"Good," the frog said. "That will do for now. Just be aware that whenever you think you know what is, that is only you thinking you know what is. It is not the truth, but a mere reflection of what might be."

"Thank you," I said.

"You are welcome," he responded very graciously. "I declare today's training complete. You may return to your distraction."

I laughed aloud at Big Frog's apparent humor at my expense. I knew this lesson had been the training I was supposed to have just then. The pollywogs had not lured me away after all. They had been a part of the lesson. The frogs knew that I had no idea about what it was to be my word. I was ripe for the distraction. The pollywogs were only the bait for a trap of my own making. I had been set up.

I stepped back to the edge of the pond and commanded, "Play with me."

In an instant, all the pollywogs were back, darting up to my finger, then away again. Every now and then, I could almost hear the laughter of playing children. I wasn't sure if I was experiencing the happy energy from the pollywogs or the sound of myself at five years of age, at the next year's fair, riding those fast and dangerous rides I had never ridden before.

CHAPTER 6

Reality and Perception

It seemed as though the temperature in the gorge had dropped slightly, but not enough to make it cold. It was late afternoon, when the sun casts long shadows across flat terrain and plays tricks with the light in the recesses of the gorge.

I sat meditating on a rock ledge just downstream from the falls, overlooking the peaceful arboretum that was the lower gorge and pond. The usually deafening roar of falling water was a far-off sound.

I was engrossed by the shadows on the upper walls of the gorge. I could swear they looked like a scene of great and powerful humans and frogs assembled together in a debate within a giant corridor. Translucent purples, blues, and reds—deep and rich—made my breath stop as I gazed at the awesome display. I wondered if it could be real.

I then became sharply aware of my own life and what had been happening recently. Here I was, in what might have been the most tranquil and beautiful spot on the planet—if it really did exist on the planet—and not one other human being knew I was here. Even though I was supposed to be on vacation driving cross-country, there was one person who expected to hear from me periodically.

I shuddered to think of the panic my wife was probably experiencing, the thoughts she must have been having about me by then—especially considering the mood of our relationship, which was the reason I had left alone on the trip in the first place.

It was clear that she loved me deeply and that she knew she had to send me away. If I truly loved her, I would come back on my own. I closed my eyes and saw her sitting across the dimly lit restaurant table, looking at me with her long, searching look.

❋　　　　❋　　　　❋

"Ted," I heard her say as I sat looking at her beautiful face reflecting the flickering light of the candle between us, "I do love you, but you really do need to go now."

We had been over it many times. This time I knew she was right. I had to go, for the sake of the marriage, and for whatever else it was that was driving me. It was time to resolve a number of things in my life.

I saw the mixture of fear and relief on her face when I finally told her I would take the time off work. I pushed away the barely-nibbled sandwich on my plate. My stomach was a pit of emptiness and remorse as I reluctantly agreed to leave her behind.

Shimmering pools danced in the bottoms of her eyes. Mine were the same as the two of us fell silent. We managed to hold the tears back, however. It wasn't the time for crying. Breathing became a chore for us both in the heavy air of the crowded, yet suddenly very lonely, restaurant.

❋　　　　❋　　　　❋

"You are thinking of your life outside of here?" a voice interrupted. The vision went away.

It was not Big Frog, but another wise frog with whom I had been recently conversing. She was also one of the larger frogs, but not so plump as Big Frog. This incredible lady frog seemed to have a degree of insight into my emotions that even the other powerful frogs apparently didn't have, or at least hadn't intimated the way she had done.

"Yes, I find myself thinking about my wife," I replied, strangely welcoming the frog's intrusion. "I don't think she was that pleased about my trip, even though she was the one who suggested I go. We've struggled in our relationship lately. I'm sure she is thinking I should have checked in with her by now. She's probably worrying."

"I detect something else from you that is, shall I say, a greater concern? I can sense that you think she might be worrying, and yet, there is something else, isn't there?"

I looked at the lime green gangly-legged creature in front of me in awe-struck admiration. Lady Frog was right. It was as though she was able to artic-ulate what I was feeling directly, as if she were feeling and distinguishing her own emotions.

"Well, I hate for her to be worrying because I'm not staying in communica-tion with her," I said tentatively.

"Yes, I can see that," she said. "And?"

"And, if I don't call her to let her know what I'm up to, she might tend to think I'm not alone, if you know what I mean."

"Ah, yes," Lady Frog said. "I could see a bit of a cloud in that area. Yet, I sense something else in you. Perhaps you are concerned that she might feel that way, and you do not completely agree with her judgment about it. Some complaint about that, I think."

My eyes shifted nervously, trying to avoid contact with the frog. My mind sorted through rampant thoughts, desperately trying to gain control, searching for a way out of the conversation.

I caught sight of something at the top of the waterfall. There was a glisten-ing there, something I hadn't seen before—a possible distraction. I tried to let my attention go to the thing, but the question before my mind would not allow it.

"I can't explain what it is, but something about her being that jealous is hard for me to accept. Her being jealous at all is hard for me to accept. It makes me feel trapped."

"Obviously," Lady Frog said. "Do you have trouble with your wife's expecta-tion that you would travel alone on this journey?"

"No, it's not that," I said. "She knew I would be alone on this trip. I can't explain it, but somehow we both knew I had to go on this trip by myself."

"Yes, we knew you were coming as well," the wise Lady Frog admitted.

My eyes went straight to hers.

"But, do you suppose that she might have understood your sudden willing-ness to leave her behind after your long refusal?" she asked.

I was more than a little surprised, and yet it seemed somewhat obvious, that the frogs knew I was coming.

"It's just that she holds onto me," I replied. "She's afraid of something. I don't know what it is, but it's as though she's afraid to let go of her hold on me. And I am afraid…well, I have a lot of trouble with her being that way."

"You do not like being held on to, do you?" she asked. "And you are com-mitted to changing that about her, aren't you?"

"I think it's more like I *need* to change her, like I know that if I don't, her jealousy will get in the way of my wanting to stay with her," I admitted. "I have committed to being with her for the rest of our lives. I am committed to her happiness and I love her. I don't understand what more I can do to make her know that. It's like there's something she wants that just can't be satisfied, no matter what I do."

"And if you could satisfy her, you would do that?" The frog pierced deeper into the place where I was protecting myself.

I looked again to the object at the top of the falls. I was once again engaged in a dialogue in an area of my life that I would rather not have looked at.

"I...I don't know. I'm not sure I can be that responsible."

"Oh, but just a moment ago you told me you were committed to her happiness."

"Yes, and I am committed to her happiness. I just don't know that I can be the one to make her happy. It's a lot to ask."

I had begun to see this as a very important inquiry.

All at once, the glistening atop the falls became airborne. My eyes followed the diversion. The object seemed to float on the air currents, gliding, soaring in slow, winding circles in its descent down toward the pond surface.

Was it a bird? No, as it drew closer I could see the form of a frog. Frogs can fly? Well, why not? I was sitting there talking to one.

"So, this conversation. Is it part of my training?" I asked.

"Yes," Lady Frog explained. "It is part of our promise to prepare you for the Great Meeting. The time for this inquiry has begun.

"You see, you think you are in a relationship with your wife. You think of your relationship as something you can shape and bend to your will, as though it were some material object. Yet, within the possibility that relationship is, there is no such substance. There is no entity one can point to and say, 'that is what a relationship is.'

"Relationship exists only as possibility, not as object. In your thinking, you have conceptualized your relationship as something that you could manage, if you only knew how. You believe this thing you call your 'relationship' should be a source of love and freedom in your life. But I ask you to consider that to experience love in relationship with another, you must be willing to be the one to bring that love into your own relating."

Lady Frog seemed to be scolding me.

I started feeling very much as I always did when my mother scolded me as a child.

Something made me think I should look to the left. I turned and thought I saw my mother standing out on the water. I blinked several times, trying to come to terms with the vision. At the same time, I tried to keep my attention on the conversation, on the scolding I was receiving from Lady Frog.

"You do not yet know that all there is to manage about your relationship is your own existence," she said. "Set aside your images of the way your relationship should unfold and operate in the naivety of not already knowing how it ought to be.

"Relationship, as possibility, is the key to our existence in the universe. Humans relate to everything as if they are separate from, rather than one with, the universe. The origin of this behavior has been communicated to you, and there is much more you will learn in your preparation for the Great Meeting, including the fact that the possibility of relationship is critical to our future."

Interestingly, when I heard the frog say 'our future' I could clearly picture humans included in it.

She continued, "We are all on this planet as one. The future for any of us is the future for us all. We are one, separate only in mind."

Attempting to bring the conversation back to my relationship, which a few moments earlier I didn't even want to look at, I said, "So, back to what we were talking about—"

"We have not strayed," she admonished. "All that is communicated here is inside of our purpose for being here."

"Okay," I surrendered, nodding my head and somehow knowing that my wish was going to be granted at a level greater than I might expect or desire.

From the corner of my eye, I saw the image of my mother fading away. I tried to reach out and catch onto her, but she was gone.

"And, looking at my commitment towards my wife's happiness, I now see that this inquiry is very important for me to engage in deeply. I'm really not sure how to be in relationship with her. If I allow her to be jealous and clinging, I think there is going to be a limit to our happiness."

"Yes," Lady Frog said. "And to what extent are your limits the limits you create yourself through your inability to be satisfied with her as she is and as she is not? What is the impact of your hypocrisy and your insistence on holding on to your own perception, depicting her as jealous and distrustful? Who are you that she is?"

"I think I've missed something." I was confused again, half expecting to see my mom return, scolding and pointing her finger. "You are saying that I am to blame for my wife's jealousy? Like I am actually giving her reasons to be jealous?"

"I did not say anything about blame or reasons, my dear human. I am merely reflecting on your inability to consider that her jealousy might exist inside of your own interpretation of your relationship, which you believe is the truth about her. Could it be that you create the world in which you live? You so resist her jealousy that you completely set aside your own love for her. You are not at all aware of her love for you. To you, she is just jealous, and you are just right about it."

Now I was really being drawn into looking at the issue. Lady Frog had gotten my attention. I knew there was power in this inquiry and I wanted all of it.

I suddenly became aware of the pounding of my heart; it was almost loud enough to hear it beating. I had a feeling of great spaciousness in the pit of my stomach. It was something other than the emptiness, which I had experienced previously in times of despair. This was a complete sense of openness, like a hunger for something powerful whose consequences I couldn't fully grasp.

"So, when you say...I mean...so, I interpret her anger towards me as jealousy, and it might not be that?"

"You interpret what you interpret, and you think it is about her," came her stinging reply. "But, what if it is about you? What if you are filtering that which she expresses through some memory from your own past? It might be a memory that may even have been a reflection of something else that happened in your life, or even a combination of events that happened long ago."

"I don't see it," I answered, perhaps a bit too quickly.

The flying frog emerged on the far side of the pond, moist and glistening. My attention momentarily shifted, and I found myself trying to figure out how such a clumsy-looking frog could glide with all that grace. I tried focusing on it from the distance to see if it had wings, picturing flying squirrels in my mind. I watched it hop, in normal frog fashion, among the rocks.

I turned my face back toward Lady Frog, but kept my eyes fixed on the shimmering mystery.

"Okay," she said, "and what if there was a particular time, long ago, perhaps when you were a child, when something happened? You may have interpreted it as someone holding on to you, or pressuring you. Due to that interpretation, you decided that it meant people will try to hold on to you. You explained it to yourself that people are attached to you and will try to hold on to you. They will take away your freedom. They will trap you."

In addition to becoming annoyed, I was starting to get the picture she was eloquently painting. I recalled a memory of my adolescence, of a girl who liked me and wanted a relationship with me. I remembered the other kids, my friends at school, laughing at me. I was embarrassed. I was really confused about that.

I actually liked this girl, but I couldn't let anyone know it because they would all laugh even more. She was persistent, leaving notes for me and telling her friends and my friends about her crush on me. Then, one day I simply had to tell her to stop.

"Leave me alone!" I said. "I don't like you."

Then something else happened. A night or two later, I was at home in my room when my mother called me to the telephone. The caller was a man, an adult. I didn't know him. He said his name was Jack and he spoke very politely. He told me I should not have treated his friend the way I did. He said I had hurt her feelings. Then he threatened me.

Jack said that he knew me and could get me before or after school any day he wanted. Listening to him frightened me more than I had ever been frightened. I felt a chill, and then a hot rush went up my back and into my neck and head, as though someone had injected hot fluid into my body. I coiled the telephone cord so tightly it nearly stretched apart.

"I have to be careful with girls," I declared to myself in a decision that would last the rest of my life.

"So," Lady Frog said. "You see something, do you not?"

I related the incident to her. She seemed to already know about it.

"It is in your design," she said. "It was the experiment. You think, and then you compare your thoughts. You experience, you interpret your experience, and then you interpret your interpretation. You make decisions about your life based on your interpretations."

I was suddenly wishing I had more control over my thinking. I saw how the experience with the girl had been affecting my marriage all these years later. I could also see how my other relationships had been shaped, and were even now being shaped, by the decision I made out of that experience.

It was affecting more than my marital relationship. It was affecting every part of my life. Whenever anyone pressed me for anything, I reacted. I protected myself.

I began to see that it might actually be okay if my wife held on to me, and that it might even be a reaction to my own tendency to push her away. I also saw how my resistance to being held had pushed others away, and how they sometimes gave up on me when they thought I couldn't be helped.

At least my wife hadn't given up on me yet. I knew that something was still possible in our relationship. Somehow, there was a chance it could turn out the way we had wanted when we got married in the first place.

"I suppose I'll have some things to say to her when I get back home."

"Yes, I am certain you will have much to talk about."

"Considering the way I've pushed her away from me, I hope she hasn't already decided to put my suitcases out on the front doorstep before I get back."

"Somehow, I think she will not do that," Lady Frog said.

"I'm going to trust that you are right about that," I said.

I was reassured by what Lady Frog had said to me. I sat and reflected for a moment, then looked up at the breathtaking site of the painted upper walls of the gorge.

I spotted the glistening flying frog again atop the falls. Once again it leaped out, gliding and soaring gracefully downward, swooping close to me, sailing away, and up, and then finally down, skimming the surface of the pond, ending in a half-circle and sinking beneath the ruffled water. It kicked a couple of times and disappeared toward the far bank.

"I don't deserve to be here," I said, as I looked over at the spot where Lady Frog had been.

She was gone.

CHAPTER 7

Traveling

The long day of rigorous lessons with the council of frogs took a fatiguing toll on me. I slowly dragged myself in the direction of the den I had become accustomed to since the night I groped my way through the dark passage.

Reaching a place where the foliage was particularly heavy, I sat down in the middle of the pathway. It had only begun to look like a path since my arrival here.

Exhausted from the strenuous soul-baring conversations, I sat still and silent with my eyes closed and my legs crossed. I leaned back against the trunk of a small white-barked birch tree and relaxed, letting go of my senses, feeling the tiredness of my body, noticing tension and even soreness in my neck and upper back. I began to mentally focus on those areas of my body, becoming hypersensitive to each sensation.

The soreness seemed to tighten into pain, then diminish rather quickly and disappear altogether. I was mildly surprised but did not allow myself to celebrate or further react to the experience. Instead, I simply noticed the sensation and then continued to explore the next area of my body.

Once again noticing pain giving way to tiredness and tension in my shoulders, and after again focusing my awareness, the sensation intensified and disappeared.

I repeated the cycle over and over with virtually every area of my body until I had become aware of a spatial feeling. My body felt light, almost as though it were floating, not grounded. I continued to notice each thought that came into my mind, but I did not react to them.

After a while, I became conscious of seeing various objects in my mind. For a moment, I wondered if I might be dreaming them. Then I regained my witnessing posture of noticing my thoughts and moving on to the next thing. I started to experience myself as being aware.

A surreal vision of a single closed eye appeared. The lid undulated with a gentle pulse of life. It seemed as though I were looking at a real human eye. The sense I had was that it might be my own eye, somehow reflected back at me.

As I continued to gaze at it, the eye appeared to reform itself into a completely different eye, metamorphosing quickly but not abruptly. It changed again and again as I watched. The skin tone and texture altered—dark, light, animal, bird, back to human.

My body jerked back as the eyelid suddenly opened to reveal a coal-black eyeball reflecting a small, whitish dot of light. I adjusted my posture and focused more intently.

Continuing to peer into the eye, I soon felt the sensation of being drawn into it, into the darkness of the pupil, into its intense blackness. I suddenly found myself inside the eye, now looking toward the reflected dot of light, feeling a new sensation of being pulled rapidly toward it.

The dot grew larger. I began to see it as more than a dot of light. Something inside the whiteness started to take shape.

As I approached, I began to see the silhouette of a human. A little closer, I saw a man standing before an assembly of other people. Closer still, I could see right through the man and into the audience of people. Closer, I saw a single face, that of a beautiful, dark-haired woman. Even closer, I saw the beautiful woman's enthralling dark eyes.

There was a flash. I was suddenly focusing again into the single eye, dark, with the dot of light reflecting. I was back at the original vision of the eye.

Again, I traveled into the image of the beautiful dark eye. I felt myself traveling great distances in the blackness of space, this time at an even greater velocity than before.

I started seeing faraway planets. At blinding speed, I was amongst them, and just as quickly beyond.

Suddenly, the passage of time shifting to slow motion, I arrived into a conversation between a woman and her child. There was no sound, but I could sense the scene was that of a scolding. The woman held a tight grip on the child's arm. The image faded.

I found myself again moving with great velocity in total darkness. Arriving finally into a group of frogs, I heard voices, many voices. I was unable to distinguish any words.

My eyes opened. I was back on the path with the strange loose-skinned frog sitting on a rock right in front of me.

I realized I hadn't seen this frog for quite some time. I looked curiously at it.

I tried to look into its eyes, but couldn't hold my gaze and instantly looked away. I could not look into this frog's eyes. I tried once more, this time with great determination. Without a single thought, my eyes looked away, automatically, as if an unseen force had deflected my gaze.

I was suddenly very suspicious of this frog. What was it doing here? Why was it in this vision? What did it have to do with my training?

CHAPTER 8

The Power of Awareness

Walking alone in the gorge during the early evening just before dark, I found myself wondering what it would be like if I were a powerful person. Whenever I had seen people who I thought of as powerful, I was always confounded at how they happened to become that way, and wondered how I could get to be that way.

I conjured up images in my mind of awe-inspiring orators commanding enthralled audiences. I pictured newspaper headlines depicting heroic leaders: presidents, generals, and corporate geniuses. I had read many books on the subject. I attended highly touted self-improvement seminars that promised to transform me into an extraordinary and powerful leader. None of them had ever addressed what I truly desired for my life.

For the most part, power always seemed to me as something others had. I longed for it, but I just did not have it.

Now, here in this obscure but potent frog village where I found myself, I couldn't help noticing that many of these frogs exuded the very kind of extraordinary power that I was interested in for myself. The more I thought about it, the more I realized that not even one of the frogs seemed to lack personal power.

I thought about the strange little frog. Even that one seemed to have a certain kind of power, maybe more so than all the frogs. I wondered if I would ever be seen as powerful.

On this particular evening, I was walking along the pathway. The day's training had been completed. The question about personal power had been lingering in my consciousness since I awoke during the night before and could not fall back to sleep.

I'd been certain most of the day that power was going to be the topic of a lesson, but it was never once mentioned by any of the frogs.

Now here I was, walking rather briskly around the circumference of the gorge, lap after lap. The frogs were buzzing around, engaged in their own activities. I hardly noticed them. They were trying to see what I was up to, but for all their efforts, they couldn't keep up with me.

My mind faintly registered seeing the strange little frog several times on the path in front of me. My awareness of the surroundings was minimal, yet I was focused to the point where I could step or leap safely without the slightest thought of endangering any frogs or myself.

At one point, a faint utterance came into my mind. It seemed to be a communication similar to that of the frogs, but it was somehow different. Strangely, I perceived the meaning of the words even before my mind consciously registered that anything had been said.

I was dumbfounded by the experience of hearing an unfamiliar phrase, yet at the same time the meaning of the utterance was mysteriously clear to me. It seemed that I knew it without having ever learned it.

Suddenly, the words of the message came again into focus. "AWARENESS," I heard in my mind. "KEY TO BEING POWERFUL."

Not knowing where the words came from, I finally just accepted that they were there. I was hearing a message, and at the same time, it seemed as though I was remembering it.

I stopped abruptly. "Oh, wait a minute," I thought. "I am hearing myself think those words."

Even with that realization, I knew it was a different kind of thinking from anything I was used to.

Awareness is key to being powerful? It made sense. I knew this wasn't the kind of awareness involved in knowing something conceptually. It was a deeper level of awareness—the kind that comes from observing and knowing.

This was profound knowing. It was the knowing of what is true, distinct from that which I believed to be the truth in my own personal reality. It was truth distinct from reality, distinct from any of my mind's limiting judgments or opinions about it.

Awareness. I suddenly knew what awareness was. It seemed as though in that moment I had unbridled access to all there was to know about everything, yet at that exact same moment I realized there was nothing I needed to know about anything.

I began walking again, more slowly this time, but just as oblivious to the physical environment. The world had become peaceful. There were no thoughts or evaluations being processed in my mind. I felt the profound simplicity and exhilaration of simply being alive.

In that moment, I knew that I was powerful, as powerful as I would ever need to be.

CHAPTER 9

Resisting Right and Wrong

I was sitting on the flat rock where I had first met the frogs. It was the place where I had been sleeping each night. My feet dangled over the edge and I was deep in thought.

It had been more than two weeks since my arrival. For the past couple of days I had been experiencing a disturbing feeling of uneasiness.

This wasn't something I had communicated about with the frogs. For some reason, I thought I should hold this in, even though for all I knew the frogs had already picked up on what was going on with me and they were just waiting for me to disclose it to them.

I had a feeling that something was wrong. I couldn't put my finger on any specific thing; it was just a deep foreboding that something was just not right here in this place.

I was caught up in my thoughts, trying to put it all together, trying to figure it out.

It seemed to me there was some kind of dangerous deception going on. Something wasn't as it should be, or maybe it was too much so, too good to be true. Was I being misled?

Maybe this whole frog community was really some ominous cabal, a group of conspirators casting spells on me to hold me in this otherwise marvelous place.

As if discourteously roused from a captivating dream by a chorus of reveille echoing through the gorge, I was pulled grudgingly to the awareness of a conversation going on near me. It took several moments before I fully realized my whereabouts and that someone was communicating with me, or trying to. I shook myself awake.

"What in your life do you resist?" I heard the voice of Big Frog coming into focus in my mind.

"I don't know what you mean," I answered, just as though we had been speaking for some time.

My eyes began to search for the frog.

"Look into your life. What about your life do you resist? What do you wish you could change? What circumstances are you avoiding in order to keep from dealing with something?"

As he asked the questions, I saw him hop out of a muddy pool. I heard the wet slap of his clumsy landing on the flat rock next to me. I was startled by the cold splatter of mucky drops of water splashing onto my bare arm.

"Well, I'm not sure," I said, wiping my hand across my wet arm and looking down at him. "Of course, there are places in my life where I'd like something to be different. I think everybody doesn't like something about the life they are living. I don't know that it means they are resisting anything," I said in defense against his accusation.

"Yes, and will you look to see if that is true for you?" The frog's question did not go away.

"I'm looking," I said, becoming slightly indignant.

"Okay, then consider those areas where you would have your life be different," he said, seemingly ignoring my indignant reply. "What do you tell yourself is wrong that you would want to be different?"

"What is *wrong*?" I asked. "I don't think anything is wrong."

My body started to take on a defensive posture.

"Why do you ask me that? Maybe something's wrong with the question you ask. You think I believe that something is wrong with my life?"

I got up and walked over to edge of the pond. I looked down and then kneeled and immersed my arm to wash off the drying mud spatter. On the way back to the rock, I reached down and pulled a fluffy white dandelion from next to the path. I was looking for something to do in case I needed a way to avoid being in the conversation, even though I already was avoiding the conversation.

"Magnificent! Let's look at that then!" Big Frog exclaimed.

The frog's demeanor seemed to change from accusatory to delight. He shifted his body and I thought he might hop onto my lap, but he stayed put.

"You claim that you do not think anything is wrong," he said. "I agree with you that nothing is wrong, yet it is you who disagrees with yourself."

I was still feeling a bit reproached as I answered.

"I have no idea where you're headed with this," I said, fidgeting. "I'm just going to trust that you are taking me somewhere, so let's just keep going and I'll try to avoid getting too upset. What do you mean when you tell me I do not agree with myself?"

"You resist the very idea that you resist. I ask very simply 'what it is that you resist,' and you resist the very question by your response. You are indignant and you fear the subject of your being indignant."

I winced as I said, "Okay, but I still don't see it. I don't see what you think I am resisting, but you must see something or we wouldn't be having a conversation about it."

I held the dandelion up to my lips and blew, watching the white down disperse and rise and fade into the sweeping breeze.

"I acknowledge and thank you for your willingness to talk with me on the subject," Big Frog said. "However, I am not yet convinced of your willingness to look into the matter of your resisting. If we continue to work you will no doubt open yourself up and we may eventually see what is there to see about that."

"Please continue," I begged, not really wanting him to.

"Thank you," he said, seeming to nod in a professorial manner. "In your design, there exist the principles of right and wrong."

"The principles of right and wrong?" I interrupted with a perplexed look.

I was intent on being open to the lesson, but at the same time, I was intent on proving that I was not resisting anything about my life.

"Yes," he went on. "In your design, there is a view of the world you are holding onto in which everything must fit into one of two categories. One is the category we will call 'right,' or 'as it should be.' The other, obviously, is the opposite category of 'wrong,' or 'as it should not be.'

"There are other ways to describe these categories. Good and bad are a subset of right and wrong, as are must and must not, need and need not. These all exist inside the design of human beings, who must classify everything as either right or wrong."

I shook my head slowly as Big Frog spoke. Maybe it was a gesture of disagreement or maybe I simply didn't want to hear the truth in what he said. I looked at him. I shrugged my shoulders in a gesture of confusion.

I said, "Okay, I'm getting that there might be something to this, but I still can't see exactly what it is you want me to get out of it. I don't see what any of it has to do with me resisting something about my life."

"Yes, and that may have something to do with your resisting as well. Perhaps we will see," the frog countered, devoid of expression, as frogs are known to be. "When you look into your life, if you truly look, do you see a place where you are not whole, where you are not completely satisfied? Perhaps there is a disagreement you have had with someone, perhaps even with yourself. Or maybe there is a circumstance in your life where it occurs to you that all is not as it should be?"

"Well, okay," I agreed, shrugging my shoulders again and raising my hands up. "But what's wrong with that?"

"I did not say anything was wrong with that," the frog said. "You, in this conversation, have been listening for something to be right or wrong. I asked you to look at where you believe something is wrong. I asked you to see where in your life you may be resisting something, where you want something to change, or perhaps you are avoiding something in the hope that it will disappear.

"You, my wily friend, have resisted the very concept that you resist anything. I am asking you to look into the possibility that, in the human design that you are, you automatically categorize every occurrence as being either right or wrong. Once you have placed something into one of those categories, you then relinquish any personal choice you have in how you will relate to it in the future."

I felt my face contort into a frown as I listened to the frog go on about how he thought I acted in my life. I wanted him to stop. I didn't know why this subject was having such an effect on me.

"You do this out of design," he continued. "It applies to everything and everyone to which or to whom you relate. The simplest, most mundane aspects of your existence are absolutely controlled by this way of being, which you inherited from your parents and from all humans before you since the time of the great separation.

"I ask you again to look into your life. See if there is an area, your relationship with your wife perhaps. Look at the place where you live, at your neighbors. Consider the people you interact with daily. See if you do not have some resistance in one of those areas to something that is not the way you think it ought to be, or to someone who has said or done something that you think is wrong. I promise that any area you consider will depict your entire life."

I pulled myself off the rock and sat down cross-legged on the path in front of Big Frog. Crossing my arms, I rocked back and forth and tapped my fingers to my lips as I mulled over the question.

"Well, I can think of some places," I said, starting to open up. I immediately thought of my wife and children. A number of my past relationships flashed in my mind. I did not want to talk about any of those.

"One place is my work," I said, "where I am accountable for the quality of service my company provides for our customers. I keep telling different agencies inside the company what the customers say they want, but no one seems to care."

I looked into Big Frog's eyes and shrugged.

"They have their own rules and policies, which don't seem to include serving our customers," I said, as if that might prove my point about the company.

"Okay," Big Frog said. "I sense that you have selected a reasonably safe area for you to look at, but we can use that for this inquiry. You will see that it is the same for even the most complex relationships of your life."

I knew there was no hiding from this frog. At the same time, I was glad he was allowing me to pick a safe area. At least, I thought it was safe. Relaxing a bit, I folded my arms across my chest. I was still more than a little worried that he had agreed on this subject so quickly.

I looked at the pond and spotted a clump of dead leaves just as they broke loose from the bank and fell into the water, starting to swirl in a slow-moving eddy.

"Would you agree that you believe that something is wrong with the way other people behave?" the frog asked.

"The people I work with? Of course," I replied. "I'm paid to represent the company to these customers and to make sure their service is better than they want and expect. We have a policy of 'exceeding the customer's expectations,' but people in our company don't even try to meet expectations," I said.

I straightened my body and stretched slightly back as I spoke, still posturing myself so as not to become too engaged in the conversation.

"And," the frog said, "you believe that they should at least attempt to fulfill on their own policy, of course."

"Of course," I said with a nod. "Where would the integrity be in saying we are going to exceed someone's expectations and then ignoring that we had ever said it? I think we already had a conversation about being our word, didn't we."

"Ah," the frog returned. "So, you do have a grievance."

"Of course I have a grievance! Doesn't it make sense?"

I was beginning to get upset with the relentless frog. I squeezed my folded arms against my ribs and looked at the clump of circling leaves. Most of them had broken out of the current and begun to slowly disperse across the surface of the pond, leaving three leaves spinning around in a tight circle.

"And would you be willing to explore your dissent right now?" the frog asked in a tone that I interpreted as demanding a response.

"Yeah, I suppose," I said, not fully aware I was becoming so irritated as we discussed the issue. I had no idea that I was looking at more than just an issue at work.

"Tell me more about your protest that you were describing. First, consider that you may believe that there is a particular way people should act when it comes to keeping promises. Look at what about their behavior is not as you believe it should be, and then tell me what your exact complaint is about them."

I thought I could see the frog bobbing up and down in emphasis as he communicated.

"Okay," I said, as I began to see what was being asked.

I lowered my head and looked directly at Big Frog on the rock.

"What is bothering me," I said, "is that they say the objective is to meet or exceed a customer's expectations, and they don't even try to do it."

Big Frog rose up and repositioned himself in front of me, lowering himself again with another wet plop.

"So," he said, "you are upset that people are not doing what they are supposed to do?"

"Well, yeah, I think so," I said, relaxing a bit.

"Now, look again at your complaint about them. There will be value in stating it exactly as it occurs for you. Certain people are not keeping their promises the way they really should?"

"Exactly. They promise service but don't deliver what they promise."

I began to feel that the frog understood what I was saying.

"So then," the frog continued, "when certain people are not living up to their promises, does it affect you?"

I looked over as two of the spinning leaves separated and began a slow orbit around the lone remaining central leaf, as though the two still thought they could resist the inevitable outward pull of the current.

"Yes," I replied to Big Frog's question, pressing my lips together tightly as I nodded slowly. "And as a result, my customers don't think I can make a difference for them. I'm the one who represents the company to them. To them, I am the company, and it looks like I'm the one not doing what I promise."

"And that has a particular impact on you as well?"

"Yes, and it makes me question how I got into that situation," I said with a frown.

"Oh, and so you might say this lament impacts in some ways on the experience of your life."

"What do you mean?"

"Let's look at it. When you put your attention on this grievance, when it is on your mind, when you are experiencing the upset of it—there are certain qualities of your life that you may not be present to, that may not even exist for you during those particular times.

"Look at what happens to you during the moments when you are aware of your upset. What is your experience right then? Do you notice any passion about your life? Do you experience any level of joy with other people? Do you sense that you are even related with those people? Do you have any level of enjoyment in your being there?"

As the frog asked the questions, I began to think about times when my complaint had arisen while I was at work. I turned my gaze toward the far side of the pond. I was recalling what it was like during those times, and how upset I'd been about the situation.

I couldn't see any joy or passion about anything in my life during those times. I remembered sometimes wanting to look for another place to work. Sometimes I actually hated working there, even though I was normally proud, and thought it was the best company to work for in the industry.

"So you could say that in those particular moments when you experienced being upset, the qualities of love, passion, satisfaction, and happiness actually did not exist in your life at all. Do you see anything else that might have been lost to you during the times you had this grievance?"

The dialogue with Big Frog was starting to break something open for me. I began to relax my posture a bit.

I looked into his eyes and said, "When I get upset about this I am completely unaware of my real commitment to the company. I might even say things to people that I don't really mean. My energy becomes focused on what is wrong. I feel drained, exhausted from my upset."

As I told these things to Big Frog, I began to notice my heels bouncing rapidly in a stressed rhythm.

"Ah, so this lamenting that you do when you are upset actually does rob you of your relationship with people, and maybe with the people you serve, and even yourself. It truly impedes the fulfillment of your own commitment. It drains your enthusiasm and your spirit."

"Yeah." I began to feel depressed and unsure of myself, paying attention now to the spasmodic disharmony of my tapping heels and my knees bouncing uncontrollably. I clasped my hands around my knees and leaned back, stretching my arms, heels still tapping. I looked at Big Frog with a concerned smile. Those other areas of my life that I didn't want to talk about were right there.

Big Frog could see I had amply seen the impact my complaining had on my life.

"And, seeing how it robs you of your aliveness," he said, "seeing that it robs you of your very life, tell me, why you would want to continue living that way? What could possibly be worth you giving your existence over to that?"

I pulled myself against my raised knees.

"Well, I don't know. It seems like it must have something to do with my level of commitment to my customers that makes me complain. I am absolutely committed to the idea of meeting or exceeding my customer's expectations. I think it's the right thing to do."

"Okay. You have a commitment to that. So what?" the frog said.

I looked at him in disbelief.

"What do you mean?" I asked.

"So what?" he repeated.

I said nothing. I just stared at him with no expression.

"Just set what you think about your commitment aside for a moment and look at it this way. Assume, for the purpose of this inquiry, that there might be something you have to gain from having this complaint, something that, to you, makes it worth keeping the complaint in existence, even though the pursuit of it makes you suffer so much."

"You think I have something to gain from being upset?" I asked with an incredulous look. I wanted to tell him he was crazy, but that didn't seem like a good idea.

"Perhaps not from the upset itself, but from holding on to the grievance that is the source of your being upset. It may be something you are not willing to let go of, and it kills your aliveness. It's something so desirable that you would actually relinquish your happiness, your fulfillment, and your self-awareness in order to hold onto that particular something. What do you suppose that could be?"

"Well, I can't think of anything that is worth all that. I don't understand. I don't think you understand."

My mind began searching for something to grasp onto. I started to rock back and forth.

"Just look and see. What makes you hold on to that complaint? What makes you be willing to get so upset that even here and now it grips you?"

"I told you. What I can see is my commitment," I said, becoming angry with him.

I dropped my hands down to the ground at my sides.

"Your commitment to meet or exceed someone else's expectations?"

"Yes!" I said with a nod and an angry look. "They're my customers. I'm there to serve them."

"Yes, and can you see that you have turned the possibility of meeting or exceeding their expectations into the right thing to do?"

"I'm not saying it's the right thing," I replied, shaking my head to make sure he understood that I was saying no. "I'm just saying people should do what they say. I do what I say, and these people are not even trying to."

"And, what does that have to do with you?" Big Frog adjusted himself again, rising up and plopping back down and splattering mud all over me again.

"I'm the one who has to face the customers," I said, chopping the air with my hand to confirm my righteousness.

"And, what does it say about you that your associates do not keep their word?"

"It means…it means," I stuttered. There was more air chopping and then my hand hung in the air as a new thought came into my mind. "It means that I am making the company wrong for not keeping their word," I said.

I started to see how I had been judging the people I worked with, yet I still was not quite ready to give in completely to the notion. I looked at the slow eddying current. All the leaves had escaped to the larger freedom of the pond. I thought about my wife asking me to leave.

"And, you are justified in your complaint, aren't you?"

"Yes, I *am*," I said in a defiant gesture, stressing the word 'am' with a raise of my head and a flip of my hand as if I were tossing something out to Big Frog.

"And, being justified about that feels really good to you doesn't it?"

"Very good," I said with a repeat of the arrogant gesture, this time replacing the head toss with an exaggerated nod.

"Like you have the answer for how it should be, and if those people would just listen to you everything would work out."

"Yes." Again, I motioned, but a little more conciliatory.

"And that feeling, the feeling of being justified in your complaint and being right and knowing that they are wrong, is that feeling worth abandoning your aliveness?"

I paused. "No way...but I guess I must have thought so."

"You have never thought so. It has nothing to do with you thinking so. It is the truth to you. You do not even have to think it. Being righteous and justified is your nature. As a sense of being, you can never allow yourself to be wrong. Humans will die for the privilege of being right. Even at times when you may concede that you might be mistaken about something, that is only an expression of you being right about your being wrong."

"Okay, I see what you mean," I said with a conciliatory gesture as I became aware of the disgust I now had for myself.

I had become clear about the cost to my life, and I had seen my own righteousness, which kept me justifying myself and giving up my freedom to it. I was suddenly confused about what to do about it.

"So, if it's my nature to be righteous, then how do I stop doing it?"

"You will not stop it," the frog admonished. "You are a human being. Now listen very closely to this. Trying to stop it would be hypocrisy, more of what you are trying to stop. There is no power in your resisting that you resist. It is your nature to resist. Resisting your nature is the very trap of your nature."

What had been disgust now turned to horror. My mind began to reel.

"So, why did you even tell me all this then?"

"You can have power by knowing your nature, much more power than you have ever had drifting obliviously along in your secret little life, making everything and everyone wrong, including yourself."

"How am I going to get this power? By getting control over it?"

"You will gain no power by controlling something. Trying to control is just another form of resisting. You will gain power when you recognize what is true about your nature. You will gain power when you see that you have no power to resist. You will gain power when you accept what is so, exactly as it is."

"Okay, now I'm really confused." I said, throwing my hands in the air.

"Yes, and your confusion becomes yet another form of your resisting, doesn't it? Being confused allows you to not be responsible for what is true about your life. It is in the knowing what is so that you can deal with what is so. You can't deal with something until you see it for what it is and what it is not."

"Knowing what is so..."

I began to look at my complaint about the company I worked for. I suddenly realized that the truth was that I was the one not being responsible for the quality of service my customer received. I was pretending to be the customer's advocate, but hiding the fact that I was deferring the whole thing to other people in the company by judging their performance as being below my standard and then resigning myself to that being the way it was.

"I am seeing something now," I said. "I was so busy making the company wrong and justifying my position about it, and the whole time I was the one holding back service to my customers. My upset was because of how I thought everyone else should be rather than really seeing where I could make the difference myself."

"Yes," the frog responded. "Now, look further into your life and see other areas where you have been resisting."

Big Frog hopped back into the mud with a resounding splash, and sloshed himself down until his legs were covered with water. He sat motionless.

I stood up and started walking toward the falls, then stopped and looked back. I saw Big Frog sitting there motionless. He seemed to be watching, measuring me. I gazed at him for a long moment.

"Thanks," I said in full voice, and turned and walked away.

CHAPTER 10

Choice and Choosing

It was deep night, or early morning. I lay awake, thinking.

Though sleep had come easily the night before, something now had my mind working hard.

"What does it mean? What does it mean?"

Whatever the question was, it was keeping me awake at this unusual hour just before the morning twilight. I was turning every few seconds, trying to find a comfortable position on the hard rock that before tonight had been my comfortable bed. How had I ever slept here these nights?

"What does it mean?"

The question kept turning over in my mind as I kept turning over on the torturous rock slab.

In the overpowering darkness, a beacon of bright light suddenly shone on an aspect of my life. A great clarity and excitement rushed into me, yet I held onto a portion of the stubborn suspicion my mind was intent on keeping.

Words came once again to me from an unfamiliar place. Unsure of the source, I wondered if God himself might be speaking to me this time. I was certain the words had not come from any of my companions in paradise, the frogs.

There seemed an uncertain familiarity about this voice. The words provoked me, yet they left me quite disturbed.

This was something else from my time in the gorge that I recall with great detail—another fact that I cannot explain. These words, that seemed to be directed at me from some obscure place, awakened me in the night:

"I wonder if you are clear that you have choice when it comes to living your life. I do not say you are not clear about it. I do assert, however, that you indeed may not be at all clear about choice in your life. As you hear these words, I invite you to consider your life as you have known it.

"If your life occurs in some particular way for you, it may be that you are living out of a set of decisions, rather than choices, that you made about yourself and about your life. It may be that those decisions now have you caught in a world where your life is throttled, a world where you have no say about how your life can unfold because you already know the way it is. You suffer the consequences of your decisions as though you have no choice.

"Consider: choice is absolute. It occurs out of discretion, but totally without reason. It is not contingent.

"You have freedom to choose once you can distinguish your concerns and commitments as the possibility that they are, and when you are bound by nothing. You are free to choose at all times, having granted yourself the freedom to choose."

As I heard and considered these words, I started thinking about choices that I had made in my life. I thought about whether I had ever really chosen anything out of freedom.

The allocution continued:

"If I say to you that I love you, I do not mean that I love you because of any particular reason. It is not because you are beautiful, intelligent, or talented. Those are attributes, features, and attractions.

"If I say I love you, it is solely a consequence of my choosing and speaking. It is what is possible becoming reality the moment I speak it. Yet, nothing remains in possibility once it is spoken.

"Possibility, once brought into existence as reality, ceases to exist as possibility. Rather, it is now a reflection of possibility. It is a memory.

"You cannot relate to possibility as memory, for that is the past. Possibility can only be accessed in the present by the committed act of choosing.

"What keeps love in possibility is the continuous act of choosing. I love you. I choose loving you. I choose you.

"Choosing is not for anything or in order to have or be or do anything. It is simply choosing.

"Choosing to love is for no reason. Choosing to not love is not choosing, since reason will always be attached to the selection.

"The avoidance of love is not choice; it is circumstance—a decision based in reason. Therefore, it follows that the absence of love is the absence of choice."

I thought about the many times in my life when I had thought that I loved someone. I realized it was really something they did or the way they looked or something that I wanted from them that had made me think and say, "I love you."

I knew there had been times when I truly was in love, but then, at some point, the experience of love always disappeared. I began to suspect that sexual attraction might have been the basis for much of what I had considered to be love in my life.

> "In the end, living your life and loving your life is a matter of choice. It is integrity, but not a matter of integrity. It is not a matter of success, or marriage, or any of what else we might think it is. It is choice. You will love your life only because you love your life when you have chosen.
>
> "When others see you loving your life, they also will want the experience of being in your life. When they see you not loving your life, their natural tendency will be to avoid being in your life. Humans have no choice in this. You will become a circumstance of their lives either way.
>
> "The nature of a human is to interpret circumstance, to define, to invent meaning. When love is present, it means all is right and the world works. When not-love is present, the world occurs as though something must be wrong. Humans cannot be with something wrong. Thus, the tendency is to love what is right and to avoid what is wrong.
>
> "Having clarity about choice will give you power to live inside of what is possible. You can make decisions based on circumstances and then live inside of your decisions. You can also choose your life and live inside your choice. Inside choice you create your world and you say how life plays out."

In a profound way, this mysterious message delivered on the wind had awakened me from more than my sleep that night. It awakened me from the insensible slumber that was my life, if only for that moment.

I fell asleep.

CHAPTER 11

Suffer to Live

The black, wet granite rocks made a jagged floor at the base of the sheer gorge wall that extended around to the waterfall. The whole area was cast in permanent shade by the enormity of the giant cypress tree growing in the space between the rocks and the flowing stream near the falls.

The proximity of the tree to the falls and the treacherous terrain on the side near the wall of the gorge made it impossible for me to walk completely around it. In thirty full paces, I could hardly walk half the circumference of this big tree's base.

Its bark was twisted and knotted with age, hanging loose, looking like the ghostly shields of an ancient legion of Spanish Conquistadors. I could walk inside the deep folds and recesses of the trunk and be completely surrounded within. Its massive limbs jutted out and up. Its boughs created a forest of dense green foliage reaching high into the sky.

I stood there, a mere speck next to the huge cypress, intent on staying cool in the mist of the falls on this unusually warm day.

The giant tree made me think of a legendary cypress tree in the Oaxaca Valley of Mexico. That ancient tree measured more than ten meters in diameter.

According to legend, The Oaxaca Tree, also known as the Tule Tree, dates to a time when men began to settle in the valley.

The beautiful tree had an underground river flowing beneath it. Animals used to gather under the tree to rest and to talk peacefully and complain about their suffering at the wickedness of men.

During that time, according to the legend, all the animals lived together and spoke the same language. The story goes on to tell how the animals were eventually conquered and killed or brought into the service of humans.

I couldn't help comparing that legend to my own experience in Master Frogs' Gorge.

I stood in the powerful, serene presence of the great tree thinking about how much I had been learning from the frogs. I reflected on what I had been told about the human emergence, wondering what might come of my new education.

Once I left this place, how would all this be put to use in the world? Should I give up my career and embark on a mission to teach others? What was really behind the frogs bringing me here and making these powerful lessons available to me? And why was it so hot on this particular day?

I suddenly became increasingly aware of the sweltering heat. It was just before noon. The day would surely get hotter by afternoon. I considered going for a swim.

"That will make me more like the frogs," I chuckled out loud.

"You move about, yet you sleep soundly," I heard someone say to me in the now-customary interruptive way.

"If you're talking about my presence of mind, I suppose I have none right now," I replied. "It is very hot today."

I pulled my shirt off.

"Is it?" The frog said to me.

This young frog was familiar to me, yet we had not interacted much to this point in my lessons. I knew him to be an extraordinary leader in the frog community and had sometimes wondered what direct interaction might occur between us.

"Are you telling me the heat doesn't bother you?" I asked as I untied my shoes.

"In what context do you consider this suffering to which you refer?" the young frog asked.

"Well, the temperature right now is nearly unbearable to me. I'm thinking about getting into the pond to cool off."

"And tell me, what is the relationship between the temperature and your being present in your life?"

"Okay, I'm thinking. All I know right now is I am burning up."

"Are you indeed?"

"Well, it's a figure of speech," I said, tugging at my left shoe and losing my balance, having to put my foot down quickly to keep from falling.

"Oh yes, in your human speech you do have such traditions, don't you?" the frog said with more than a touch of sarcasm.

"Well, yeah," I replied. "But I sense that you are going to give me some alternative, aren't you?"

"Perhaps I will give you nothing and you will have your alternative," he said curiously.

"What is the subject of this training?" I asked, sitting down to pull off my shoes.

"Ah, and do you notice that you are suddenly present?"

"Uh, I suppose so," I said, smiling, suddenly realizing that I had not been aware of the heat for those few seconds, but then I was again.

"Yes," he said. "You were. And what do you suppose changed in that moment when you became present?"

"Well," I answered. "I was engaged in our conversation and I wasn't thinking about the heat."

"So, are you saying that you were not suffering from the heat?"

I stopped. "I...I...guess I was not suffering from the heat."

The slender young frog abruptly leaned his head to the right and hopped almost sideways into the pond, producing an ungraceful plopping sound as he belly flopped against the water.

I watched him glide skillfully and then kick as he disappeared into the darkness of the tannin-rich water. My gaze was broken a moment later when a large solitary bubble rose to the surface and burst, its gaseous contents escaping into the open air.

It was clear to me that this conversation about suffering in the heat was important, and it was my lesson just then. I felt completely different, no longer suffering the heat, somehow powerfully engaged in the process of being alive.

My body felt vital and strong. The air I breathed seemed more nourishing, more satisfying to my lungs. My heart beat powerfully in my chest, but not as when I had been frightened that first night. Maybe it was exactly that way, but with the excited anticipation that one has when possibility becomes rich.

I felt in tune with myself, unconcerned about what anything meant. I was simply in the inquiry of life itself.

Standing in that garden of paradise, I was keenly aware of the conversation I'd just had. I thought about the physical environment around me, and about the suffering I had experienced and let go of. I didn't know how that had happened, but I knew there was still something powerful available I could take from this experience.

"This is a very powerful experience, yet I think there is something else to get at here." I said to Big Frog, who I knew was not nearby.

"Yes, there is more," he replied immediately.

I was surprised but not shaken to hear Big Frog reply.

"I am interested that we are communicating just now. I somehow knew that we could, even though I don't think you're near me. It seems natural that we can talk at a distance. It also seems appropriate that this is happening right now."

"It is very appropriate," Big Frog said.

As I heard these words, I saw a vision of him perched in the shade beneath a broad leaf next to the stream at the opposite end of the gorge. It was as if I were sitting directly in front of him.

He continued, "I observed the shift in your being when you became present a moment ago."

"I have two questions. First, are you suffering in the heat?" I asked jokingly.

"Ah, very observant," came his reply. "I am managing the well-being of my skin."

I could tell he saw my humor.

"And, what is your second question?" he asked.

"Was there any reason why the young one leaped into the water at the end of our conversation?"

Just then, I caught sight of the younger frog surfacing and watched him climb onto the tip of a stone that jutted from the dark water near the base of the cypress tree.

"What makes you believe that the conversation was over?" Big Frog asked.

"Ah!" I exclaimed, "So it was your plan to step in at this point?"

"You spoke to me, and thus we are conversing. You conversed with the other and thus you are in an inquiry. A question was asked which began a vibration, which resounds still."

"What question was that?" I asked.

"I will restate the question, though I hear it yet in your being," Big Frog said. "By all that suffering is and by all that suffering is not, the question was this: 'In what context do you consider your suffering?'"

"I see. I didn't realize that was the question."

"You did not realize that it was the question and yet the question remains. You are in this conversation, where you may stand inside the question and see what you may see."

"In what context do I consider my suffering?" I repeated. "Now, I suppose we've talked about suffering before.

The inquiry into suffering, or the context of my consideration of suffering, wasn't something I had any particular desire to undertake. It was not that I wasn't interested. It was more that I had no idea where to begin to consider it from. Nonetheless, the assignment was there, whether it was clear to me or not.

I began by looking into my life and trying to recall times when I had suffered. I noticed a few small frogs had joined me under the cypress tree, as though an audience was forming for my benefit. Perhaps they came in amazement that I was standing there communicating with Big Frog, who was elsewhere. I certainly was amazed about that. Another few frogs emerged from the pond among the gigantic roots.

"I suppose the most suffering I have experienced involved leaving my children when my marriages failed," I said.

"What happened?" Big Frog asked.

"With my two oldest it actually happened twice. Once was when I had taken them and their mother to the airport. The children had no idea why I was not going with them.

"'Can't you come with us, Daddy?' my three-year-old daughter had asked.

"'No,' I had told her. 'I'll be coming later.'

"That was the temporary separation that led to the permanent separation between my wife and me. I recall the beginning of the conversation she and I had after I had decided they should all go away.

"I started out with some comment about how our relationship just wasn't working. I don't recall what I said to justify it to her. I know that I did not tell her it was because I wanted to be single and make myself available for someone else."

"That might be an interesting conversation for another time," he said. "What else happened?"

"Well, after they left, I didn't really feel very available. I knew I was wrong and that what I did had broken all of our hearts. I justified it to myself and others by saying we wanted different things and we weren't compatible."

"Yes, you were single and she was not."

"Precisely," I said. "But I was not available for long. Very soon after, I began living with another woman.

"I fell in love with her. We played and did everything together. We traveled around the countryside and went to fun places. I know now that I used that time to avoid being responsible for what I had done to my family.

"A year later, I rejoined my family in California. The other woman was by then carrying my child and waiting for me to say if I was going to stay with my first family or stay with her.

"I desperately wanted to be responsible and keep my family together. I also had a dilemma concerning my new family.

"It didn't take long for me to find out that I couldn't live with what I had done and stay with my wife. So, I again took the easy route and told her it just wouldn't work for us to be together. I left again. My wife's tough and angry reaction made it easier that time.

"Saying goodbye to my children caused me great sadness. I will never forget the way my daughter looked at me as I left. Her innocent stare followed me as I turned the car around and drove away. I can still see her watching me when I close my eyes. It broke my heart."

"Tell me about your broken heart," he said.

"It was as though I died in that moment, that moment when I broke my daughter's heart. My marriage was a failure. My life was a failure. I didn't know if leaving was the right thing to do. I was beginning something that was completely unrecognizable and unpredictable."

"And yet, you did leave."

"Yes, I did. I left my family and went to begin a new one. Then, after a few years, that marriage failed too, when I started to seek that feeling of freedom again. This time I was not the one who left the family, but I was still not willing to take responsibility for my life. In many respects, I was already gone before she took our two children and left me. Now I truly was a failure, and I was devastated."

"You suffered greatly," Big Frog said with empathy that surprised me.

"Yes, I became quite cynical about my life. For a while, I threw myself into my work, but even that eventually became empty for me. It was as though I had no reason to move forward. As I am saying this, I can't recall anything about that time that was anything more than merely existing, surviving."

"So, you were really suffering, weren't you?"

"Well, yes. I was suffering. My whole existence became going to work and coming home, shopping for groceries and then coming back home, paying my bills and suffering. It was all suffering."

"When did that change?" Big Frog asked.

I began to get annoyed with his questions. I noticed Lady Frog coming out of the water.

"It stopped when I met the woman who is now my wife," I said, watching Lady Frog position herself in some tall grass. "She inspired me to be alive."

"Ah, so it is she who is responsible for your being alive."

"No, well, but if it weren't for her—"

"No, well, but if it weren't for her you would be still suffering."

"The point is that I fell in love with her and my life took on new meaning. I stopped suffering because I had something to look forward to at the end of each day."

"No," Big Frog said, as I thought I heard him bellow deeply in the distance.

I saw the other frogs become tense.

"The point is," Big Frog said, "that you suffer to the level of whatever circumstances you are facing at any particular moment in your life. If the weather turns cloudy, you suffer the loss of the sun. If you are late for an appointment, you suffer over how it makes you appear to others. If you are lost in the fog, you suffer over your confusion. If you have nothing to suffer about, you suffer the meaninglessness of your life, and then you suffer because you are suffering. You live your life either in the mode of suffering or in the mode of not suffering. The context of your life is suffering."

"Oh, and I suppose that I should not have suffered when I broke the hearts of my wives and children?"

"Did your suffering cause you to be responsible for what you had done? Did your suffering cause you to be responsible for your life?"

I fell silent. Big Frog's questions dumbfounded me. All of the frogs went still as stone. My mind stopped working—seized.

"Darling human, where have you gone?" Big Frog said in a gentle, low-pitched hum. It nudged my attention.

I began to regain myself. "I am here. I apologize. I don't know what just happened."

"What happened was that the question pierced the unbearable lie that consumes your life," he responded.

"I believe you're right," I replied with a sigh. "But, I don't know what to do with that."

"What to do is to go deeper into this inquiry. You may want to stop now. You may be suffering in this moment.

"This is where you may break through what stops you living your life. You are standing in a place of unrecognizable possibility. It is a place of non-existence and non-identity, where you may literally bring forth your self as a possibility through your speaking."

"So, I have lived to suffer."

"You have suffered to live."

"Your humor shows up at some very strange times," I told him. "It looks like I held onto the suffering in order to justify not being responsible for the horrible things I had done in my life."

"You could say it that way," he said. "There is no telling if the circumstances of your life would ever have been different. Coming from the place you came from, suffering to prove how good you really are, there was no possibility of being responsible and bringing completion to your circumstances. It was your circle of incompletion that made you suffer, and your suffering kept your circumstances incomplete."

"And the pretense that I based my suffering on masked the fact that I was not being responsible for the unholy jerk I had been to people in my life, to my family. I was always acting like someone who cared but staying completely aloof, judging and discounting everyone and who they all were."

"Yes," he said. "And, pay close attention to this: what you must do now is speak yourself into existence as possibility."

"How do I do that?"

"Declare yourself. Say who you are in the matter of your life," he commanded. "Recall our conversation about being your word. I asked you who you are that you are."

"Yes, I remember it."

"I want you to do more than remember. I ask you to bring it into your awareness so that you may consider it as you invent the possibility for your life."

"Okay, I have it. I said I am that I am."

"Yes."

"So, I am going to declare that I will no longer suffer in my life."

"Yes, and how do you suppose that will turn out?"

"It doesn't look good, does it?" I said.

"Now your humor has returned," he said. "In declaring yourself as a possibility, you will want to bring forth that possibility powerfully into existence. Your speaking it is the key its power," he said.

"So, I declare myself as being responsible for everything I do and have done."

"That's not bad," the frog said. "But, what if you state it a more powerful way? Try saying that you are the possibility of being responsible."

"Okay," I responded. "The possibility of being responsible."

"Don't repeat it. Declare it."

"I declare myself as the possibility of being responsible."

"Who are you?"

"I am the possibility of being responsible."

"Are you inspired to be that possibility?"

"Oh, yes," I answered with a quiver. "I am inspired. I'm inspired to get busy cleaning up the mess I've made of my life."

"I believe you may be inspired," he said. "You have brought clarity to the context of your suffering and you have invented a new possibility in which you can stand inside and live your life. I declare this conversation complete."

I was standing in the exact spot where I had been at the beginning of the conversation. I watched Young Frog again lean to his right and slip, this time more gracefully, into the water, gliding and kicking and finally disappearing again into the darkness.

It was a gloriously hot day. I stood in the mist with my face to the sun. The heat was a joy against my tight skin. I dove into the dark pool at the base of the cypress. I found the water to be very deep as I kicked and glided. The water was icy cold, and it felt great.

That evening I sat by the edge of the pond, still tingling with the possibility I had invented for my life. Pulling a small tablet and pen from my backpack, I wrote down the words to a song that had been forming in my mind.

> *When I was young, I used to play out in the rain*
> *Until Mom would call me in*
> *Sometimes I'd look up at the night sky*
> *And the stars would be my friends*
>
> *But I've seen writing on the surface of the moon*
> *And I suffered with it so*

I cried, I whined, I whimpered
'Cause what it meant I did not know

Have you ever looked at the full moon?
Perhaps you know what I have seen
Was something there would you tell me please?
What, oh what did it mean?

Come to me in my dreams
Transcend the distance of my mind
If happiness is my birthright
Then why do I deny

Oh there's the writing on the surface of the moon
And I suffer with it so
I cry, I whine, I whimper
'Cause what it means I do not know

Give my possessions to my children and my love
If I should leave them all behind
Oh, give my love to all the people of the world
Transcend the distance of my mind

Break my heart if you think you can
Or love me 'cause you say you do
Either way, I'll have my pain
And, it's not because of you

See the writing on the surface of the moon
Do not suffer with the sign
There's no meaning in the writing that you see
Transcend the distance of your mind

CHAPTER 12

Responsibility: Four Dimensions

The shadows receded to the underbrush as the sun made its late "Kilroy was here" appearance over the high cliffs.

I'd been walking most of the morning, thinking again about what all of this preparation meant. With my hands clasped behind my back, I strolled and wondered how I could give what I was getting here to the human beings of the world where I came from. How could I have it myself if I could not give it away to others? I was still not certain that I accepted it as reality anyway. I wasn't really sure I could accept even the possibility of it.

"What would it be like if you were actually responsible for all that was, all that is, and all that will be?" I heard the familiar voice of Big Frog say.

"You mean, if I were really responsible for everything—past, present, and future?"

I turned to face him sitting on a broad lily pad square in the middle of the pond. Lady Frog sat next to him, though she showed no intent to join the conversation.

"Yes," he replied. "What would that be like? Can you even consider it?"

"Well," I began to respond. "I would...I...well, it would be...I suppose we're going to have a discussion to find out what it might be like."

"Ah, but you did want to answer straight away, didn't you?"

"Well, it seems like—and I know this is not what the question is about—but it seems like I want to defend something, like that I am responsible already," I said, as honestly as I could.

I stepped slowly to the edge of the pond, my hands still clasped behind me. I looked down at my reflection in the pond.

"Yes, and to some extent, you are responsible, aren't you?" Big Frog said. "Perhaps you are not clear on what being responsible really is."

"Oh, I knew it was going to be something," I said, throwing my hands up. "I've been walking around here all morning with this ominous sense that something was about to happen, that my world was about to change."

"I have been aware of your trepidation. And it is appropriate. In this conversation, we shall see a new paradigm emerge for what it is to be responsible."

"A new paradigm...good," I said. "How shall we begin?"

I kicked off my shoes and rolled up my pant legs, watching the two frogs on the pond as I sat on the bank and lowered my feet into the icy water. A chill went up my spine and into the back of my neck. My face contorted as my body tightened and shivered.

"We have begun already," he replied. "The question was asked. What would it be like if you really were responsible for all that was, all that is, and all that will be? Now, the question itself does not reveal the whole inquiry. It is a starting point from where we can begin to look at the entire abstraction of responsibility."

"What do you mean by 'abstraction?'" I asked.

"Abstraction, as in considering a quality apart from anything which possesses it. One might say that the sky is blue, but does one consider the quality of the sky's blueness? Does one consider blueness at all?

"One might also consider responsibility as a quality like blueness. Either can be possessed, yet is capable of being considered apart from that which possesses it. Most humans do not consider the quality of responsibility abstractly. Humans are dominated by the notion that they are responsible, yet in practice they resist responsibility as a desirable quality. Did you not say you already are responsible?"

"Well, yes, and I knew when I said it that I would find out something different."

I snapped my leg straight, lifting my foot out of the water with a splash toward the great frog coach. There was a noticeable resounding kerplunk as my foot went back under the water.

"We will move on," Big Frog declared, seemingly satisfied with my reply. "If you were able to visualize the model of existence by which humans define themselves, what you might see is that it is a structure with two dimensions, based on the two concepts of problem and solution. Can you see that?"

"Well, let's have some examples," I replied, having no idea where he was going.

"For example, in the case of how humans manage their health and well-being," the frog began. "Is it not based in the notion that in order to be well, a human must not be ill or injured?"

"That seems pretty obvious," I said, pulling my feet back toward me until only my toes were submerged.

"And, along with that, is there not a certain amount of worry about the possibility of being ill or injured?"

"I think so, but I don't necessarily see that as problem and solution."

"When you are sick, do you have a problem to solve?"

"Yes."

Lady Frog suddenly turned in my direction and looked as if she might speak. She remained silent.

"And, if you are injured, do you have a problem?" Big Frog asked.

"Yes."

"Can you not then see that the way of relating to sickness and injury is, for you, an exercise in either solving problems or avoiding problems?"

"Okay, I can see that, I guess. But I'm not sure where this whole thing is going," I said with a tone of rejection.

I gently tapped the bottoms of my feet against the pond's surface, creating a rippling set of concentric circles. The one on the right was the more pronounced and longer lasting.

"Perhaps you can now see that this type of existence is indeed a flat, two-dimensional existence, where solutions are always reactions to problems or to expectations of problems?"

"That seems right," I said, still holding on to my confusion.

"And, what occurs in that model of existence," Big Frog said, "is a position. A solution is a reaction to a problem. A particular solution becomes the right solution for a particular problem. The avoidance of a problem is, of course, always the best solution."

After a short pause, Big Frog went on. "There is not much room for other possibilities once one has taken a position about a particular solution, is there?"

"I don't think so."

"So then," he said, "do two-dimensional problems and solutions offer much in the way of possibility?"

"No, it doesn't seem so."

"And if one were to combine with those two a third dimension that we will call accountability, what might be possible?"

"Accountability?" I asked. "I'm not sure." I began to see more frogs appearing in the vicinity.

"Consider that the ability to account for the truth about the whole problem-and-solution paradigm adds another dimension of being to the model."

"So, let me see…there is a world of problem and solution. If I am able to account for what is true about that, the model gets transformed into a three-dimensional model of existence. I'm starting to get a picture of something, but I have no idea what yet."

"We have now reached a place to begin to inquire," Big Frog stated.

"Oh, I've heard that one before. That means it's time for me to get to work," I said. "And I see the audience is growing."

I waved my hand in acknowledgement of the assembly of interested frogs.

"Yes," Big Frog replied. "But, it is a kind of work that you enjoy, isn't it?"

"Yeah, maybe after I have the work behind me," I replied with just a hint of sarcasm.

"Then, what else do you see about being responsible?"

"Well, we began by speaking of responsibility and diverged into these models of existence. I finally understand the conversation about problems and solutions and I can even see that there's something about accountability that might move it from two dimensions to a three-dimensional model.

"In my mind, I can picture problem-solution as occurring on a flat plane, like a photograph or a painting or as a reflection in this pond. Graphically, I see problems as existing on one axis and solutions on the other. Bringing in accountability would give the picture depth, and that's what makes it three-dimensional. It almost seems to make sense, but then it seems like there's something else that we haven't looked at yet."

"Good. What else could there be?"

"Okay. I can account for the trap of being positional. I mean, that seems to clarify whether or not existence consists of problems and solutions. I seem to have some choice when I acknowledge having a position in the matter."

"Yes?" Big Frog seemed to sit up higher in response to my comments.

"But, I still think it's incomplete, like there's something that we're leaving out."

Lady Frog suddenly disappeared beneath the lily pads.

"What is it that you think might be missing?" Big Frog asked.

"Well, this might sound weird, but—all of it. Like, the whole thing," I replied.

"And where does 'weird' occur?"

"In my own thinking, I'm sure."

"Of course, and what is the existence of that?"

"Problem-Solution."

"So, can you allow it to be weird and stay in the inquiry?" he asked.

"Yes," I said. "I can also see that this would be the place where I would normally stop looking."

"And, by your noticing that, what happened?"

"It shifted into the three-dimensional model of existence," I said with excitement.

I stood and walked toward a rock as though I was going to sit on it, but then walked back to the edge of the pond and sat back down.

"What else do you see?" Big Frog asked.

"I see that I have more power to deal with this inquiry now that I have accounted for the weirdness of it."

"Anything more?"

"There's still something missing. It's like, yes, I can account for or acknowledge something and gain the power to deal with it. Yet, it's still a reaction to something. I'm still reacting to a problem. I may be able to get unstuck from my position about it temporarily, but I'm still trying to fix things, which just eventually puts me right back into a position about it."

"So, you are saying that three dimensions may not be sufficient for dealing with all of that?"

"I think that's what I'm saying," I replied quickly. "It's like what's missing is something that ties the whole thing together."

I used my hands to make a motion in the air, like encircling a non-existent globe.

"What could tie all that together?"

It suddenly occurred to me that there might be another dimension that we had not looked at.

"When I picture problem and solution graphically with the problem being fixed at one axis and the solution being the second axis, I see that only one flat plane of existence can be considered."

I spread my hands in a poor imitation of a mime feeling the inside of an imaginary box.

"By adding the third dimension of accountability, the model of existence takes on depth."

I encircled the globe again.

"But, what I also begin to see as missing is the dimension of time."

I waved my hand from left to right as if that were the symbol of all encompassing time.

"I can see that time might tie the whole thing together, but I am not sure how it all fits," I said, and then paused. "I believe it has something to do with time."

"Ah, time. That is very interesting. Tell me more about that," the frog said, as Lady Frog clumsily climbed onto another lily pad nearby.

"Well, I don't know, but I'll keep rambling and we'll see what happens. If it is time, then how can I bring time into the model?"

I became silent, though I was not expecting anything from the frog. I thought a moment and began to speak again.

"If time consists of the past, the present, and the future, then my accounting must include all of that at once. But, I would still be dealing with it as a reaction to something. So, what else is there that could encapsulate it all with the dimension of time?"

"You are starting to see something," the frog replied. "Stay with that."

"It's not enough to just account for it over time. I must...I must..." I became silent again. "I must take responsibility for it!" I threw my hands into the air, elated, though I still didn't quite have it.

"Ah, yes!" Big Frog exclaimed. "We are back to responsibility, aren't we?"

"Of course!" I said. "We began this conversation about responsibility! I got wrapped up in the elements of it and forgot. By first accounting for it all, including the temporality of it, what is left then is to simply take responsibility for it inside of all temporality. Taking responsibility for what was, what is, and what will be allows for a different level of freedom than simply solving a problem. It makes what is possible outside of the current reality available!"

"Yes, I believe you have invented a four-dimensional model of existence where being responsible for all that was, all that is, and all that will be allows for the possibility of being at cause in the world that is created by you. Operating inside this model of existence, you are cause in the matter, rather than an effect of, that which you create."

Lady Frog seemed to study my eyes for a moment and then hopped off her pad back into the water. Many of the frogs that had been witnessing the exchange moved closer to me and seemed to look into my eyes and then they all crawled or hopped away.

Big Frog sat motionless on his lily pad, as would any normal frog not acknowledging the presence of a human that posed it no threat.

I clasped my hands behind my back and walked away, smiling and shaking my head.

CHAPTER 13

The Possibility of Possibility

It had been a wakeful night of disquieting anticipation. A question kept turning over in my sleepless mind.

"What is the possibility of possibility? What is the possibility of possibility?"

That question finally got the better of me. Reluctantly, I decided to get up, rubbing my tired and burning eyes.

"Is it time to come to the meeting place?" I asked, thinking the sleeplessness might be a summons to a lesson.

The only answer was an eerie silence. I sat up and looked around, but saw nothing in the darkness. My weary eyes could not read the face of my watch. It was that part of the middle of the night, it seemed, when even the nocturnal creatures stop stirring. Still the question played in my mind.

"What is the possibility of possibility?"

I lay back down but remained awake, pondering the significance of the question. I was actually rather intrigued, finally asking myself the question aloud.

"What is the possibility of possibility?"

At some point I fell back to sleep with the question still there, waking later to scattered spears and arrows of light filtering through the trees, showering down on me.

An incredible peace was noticeable around me. It seemed to me that I was alone. Nothing moved within my sight or senses.

I arose and stretched. I had a feeling of discomfort that I couldn't understand. After a few minutes of light stretching to wake up my body, I started to walk along the pathway, stopping from time to time to ponder where the frogs could be, though I was not really concerned about them.

I kneeled down and took a drink from the stream that fed the pond, rolling up a large rubbery leaf into a cone, pinching the bottom and dipping it into the cool running water and putting it to my lips.

"Ah," I thought. "Sometimes water just tastes so good."

As I approached the loud sound of the falls, I began to notice the frogs had positioned themselves in various places all around the pool. Each was facing toward a pointed end of a leaf or a protruding shoot of a plant. They sat motionless, seeming to stare at the lowest protruding point of the leaf or shoot.

On closer examination, I could see that each frog had focused its gaze on a single droplet of water poised in front of it.

"What are you all doing?" I asked.

The whole community shuddered with movement as my question resounded in the collective Anouran consciousness. They all eventually settled back into what they had been doing, or not doing as I perceived it at the time.

I heard Big Frog say calmly, "We are looking into the possibility of possibility."

"What is the possibility of possibility?" I heard myself ask.

"Indeed," came the reply.

Big Frog turned to look at me while the others remained fixed.

"Come," he said. "We shall look into the possibility of possibility together."

He had me stand facing a large, moist leaf.

"See the droplet?" he said. "Look into the droplet and tell me what you see."

"I see the clearness of the droplet." I answered. "What should I see?"

"It is not what you should see," he coached. "Look at what is there."

"I'll probably need some help with this," I said.

"Yes, your eyes will only see what your mind allows," he said. "And there is so much that you do not yet see. It is now time for you to step beyond your mind's limits into the possibility of possibility. The entire world in which you have lived to this point is a world that you created separate from the possibilities outside of the temporal language of your mind. Now consider that there is more than you ever imagined, even in that single droplet of water."

I turned my face in the direction of the frog, keeping my eyes on the droplet.

"I have been aware that more is possible than what I already know," I said.

My comment was an attempt to convince Big Frog that I had remained open in my life.

"Being aware of more possibility is a possible way to be. We are looking into the possibility of possibility itself. You do not define possibility as that of which you are aware. Rather, possibility is that and all else of which you have no occurring, of which you are not aware.

"Now, look into the droplet and see the possibility of possibility, for all that may be dwells inside of all space and inside of no space. The possibility of possibility exists inside that very droplet and inside each particle of that droplet and in all droplets and in all that is."

"I am looking into the droplet. I see the reflected images of things around the droplet. I see the reflected image of myself. I see your reflection…"

"Yes, and continue to focus," Big Frog said. "What else do you see?"

"I see the transparency of the droplet. I see the color of the leaf through the droplet…"

"And, do you see into the droplet itself? What is there inside the droplet?"

"I can't…see…"

I was struggling to get my mind around the task.

"Remain here looking into the droplet. When you are no longer here, you may see the possibility of possibility. When you have seen the possibility of possibility you will have gained all there is to gain from this lesson."

Big Frog left me there, standing in that ridiculous position, looking at a silly drop of water on the tip of a leaf, my head torn over whether or not I should obey the instruction.

Holding my gaze on the droplet, my mind strayed to all manner of subjects. I checked my surroundings on several occasions to verify that I was not in this pursuit alone. Each time I looked, I saw all of the frogs fixed in their own meditative inquiries about the possibility of possibility.

Interestingly, I began to sense a kind of communal power that seemed to be feeding into me and passing through me and back to the community. I began to experience comfort in being in this inquiry with the frogs.

After a while, I started seeing my thoughts as they passed through my mind. I saw faces, or parts of faces—eyes, lips, ears. I began to see varying shapes and colors, objects that looked like highly magnified cells in motion—shifting, growing, dividing.

There was darkness so dark it looked like a void, and there was light so bright that my eyes wanted to squint. My mind distinguished picture after picture inside that tiny drop of water.

I pondered each scene until I was certain there was no lesson in it for me, or until the scene gave way to the next. A wide range of emotions came over me as

I stood there. I felt humor and laughed. I felt sadness and cried. I saw grave injustices and despair, great opportunity, touching acts of kindness. I saw family and community, desperate loneliness and pitiful bad luck.

I saw the wholeness of life in that tiny droplet, great fortune and tragic necessity, unreal terror, and infinite other concepts.

After an undeterminable amount of time, my mind stopped doing what it had been doing. I simply began to be with the droplet of water in such a way that I was able to see what truly was before me.

In one moment, there was all that stuff I had been seeing. In the next, there was all that was. I saw the droplet of water. There was nothing else there.

The droplet was only a droplet, nothing more, nothing less.

In that instant, I felt the collective sigh of the entire frog community.

Big Frog communicated, "Yes. It is a drop of water. What we have been contemplating is what we see. It is a drop of water."

He then spoke to me, "Thank you for inquiring with us. We have all shared in this breakthrough in being. We all have seen that a drop of water is only a drop of water.

There is no meaning in a drop of water regardless of what our minds see. We might interpret that it contains our very lives, yet it remains nothing more than a drop of water. What was the lesson you learned from this exercise?"

I opened my eyes wide and shook my head as though I'd experienced something unbelievable.

"The lesson I learned was that a drop of water is a drop of water, and that is all it is. A drop of water has no inherent meaning. What I got out of this exercise is that a drop of water doesn't mean anything. Everything that has ever happened in my life is like that drop of water. I made up all the meaning in my life. I saw that possibility has no meaning."

"The droplet contains all that is possible, yet it remains a droplet of water," Big Frog stated.

"I have lived my whole life inside of the meaning that I placed on the droplets of water in my life," I said.

I took a deep breath, held it, and then let it go.

"Yes, you have."

I saw the frogs turning away from the leaves, going back to their normal activities. Most of them went straight for the pond.

"You know," I said to Big Frog, "I did see the possibility of possibility, didn't I?"

"You did indeed, my friend."

Big Frog turned and hopped to the edge of the pond.

"We all saw the possibility of possibility," he said. "Thank you for sharing it with us."

He gracefully pointed his nose into the water and his heavy body followed. He kicked once and made a wave in the water just below the surface. Another kick of his powerful legs and he was gone into the shadowy depths under the rocks.

I wished I could follow him.

CHAPTER 14

Transformation

"Can you be responsible for whatever you have transformed in your life?" Lady Frog asked me.

"What do you mean?" I asked in my usual confused tone. "I think I can be responsible for it, but I am not certain about the context of your question."

"It is merely a question," Big Frog said, as he appeared on a wet rock next to me and inserted himself into the conversation. "As the droplet of water was but a droplet of water, a question is only a question in the context of inquiry."

"Yes, I understand that. I'm looking at what the question is asking me," I said, sitting down.

I swung my bare feet into the cool pond and lay back on one elbow, looking at Big Frog.

"I haven't seen anything yet," I said.

"You have transformed certain aspects of your life, haven't you?" Lady Frog asked from her lily pad perch a few feet away.

"Yes, I have—and recently."

"And the question is, can you be responsible for the change, and for keeping it alive?"

"Well, yes," I said, shrugging my shoulders.

I thought I knew the right answer.

"Okay, then tell us about that."

Lady Frog's challenge caught me by surprise. I looked dumbfounded at her.

"Well, I don't know what to say," I began in struggle. "You asked me if I could be responsible. I said I could and now you want me to say something about that."

I thought I could detect a smile on both their faces as I started to fidget. I sat up trying to hide my own embarrassed smile.

"Do you know, human, that transforming one's relationship to one's self, as wonderful as that might seem, will not itself sustain beyond the memory of it?" Big Frog spoke. "It is not enough to merely experience a transformation and to relegate it to memory. One must continue to transform one's relationship to one's self. When one stops doing so, one lives in a story about one's life rather than in the experience of it."

"I'm starting to get something here," I said, drawing my feet out of the water and clasping my hands around my knees. "I can see there are some things to be responsible for. But first, I think, I have to account for what has happened."

"Yes?" Lady Frog said, anticipating me.

She seemed to draw closer, though she never left her lily pad.

"Well…" I searched. "I'm thinking there must be more to account for than just knowing that something was transformed. I not only have to account for what happened, but also for what is happening. I have to understand the entire experience and feel its impact on my life."

"Say more," Big Frog said with interest.

He shifted onto his feet, raising his body up from the rock as he turned himself and faced me directly. There was a squishing sound as he plopped down again.

"Well, it isn't enough to just record that something has changed and then say 'Oh yeah, that happened.' To really be able to account for something and be responsible for all of it, I need to actually experience it, to know and understand how it affects my life, to understand it as a reality."

"What do you mean when you say 'all of it?'" Big Frog asked.

"Well…what I said. What happened before and what is happening right now."

I had begun throwing words at the issue hoping to stumble onto something. I wasn't aware of it, but the technique actually seemed to be working.

"Is that all there is to be responsible for?" Big Frog asked.

"I'm looking," I replied. "Being responsible for what happened…the past…what is happening now…the present…wait!"

I thought about the lesson of the four-dimensional model of responsibility, as though it had been a long time since we'd had that conversation.

"I can be responsible for the future that is going to happen," I said with a smile.

"Ah," Big Frog exclaimed. "You can be responsible for what was, what is, and what will be."

"Yes!"

I was excited, but over what I was not sure. I stood up and realized I didn't intend to go anywhere. I sat back down.

"So, what does that give you regarding the question of being responsible for that which you have transformed in your life?" Lady Frog abruptly asked, disrupting my celebration.

"Well…" I said, struggling again.

"What do you see?" she asked.

"I see that I have experienced transformation in certain areas of my life, but I am not always conscious of it for very long after. Maybe I don't really allow myself to experience it," I replied.

"Go on," Lady Frog commanded in a gentle way.

"Well, it seems like what I have thought is that once I've had an experience of shifting something in a particular area, that was it. I was done with that, time to go on to the next thing.

"When I saw what was possible in my relationship with my family, I was so excited about going back and having this great life, but what I'm noticing now is that I have started to live as though that is going to be there when I get home, like the transformation I saw will just be that way now. I can see that even right here with you I am comparing my insights to my memories of transforming something before, and I have the expectation that I'll be able to make it happen that same way again.

"Whoa! Wait a minute!" I said. "I see something else."

Suddenly, I had a feeling of sadness. My feet dropped back into the water. I pressed my hands tight against my face, covering my eyes.

"I actually try to make the future happen based on memories of my experiences from the past. Like if I just do that again, everything will be great, or if I avoid that, everything will be fine the next time."

"And what is your sadness about?" Big Frog asked.

"I just this moment realized that the memories of my experiences don't equal experiencing something now or creating the future. I had no idea I was even doing that."

I took my hands away and looked disbelieving at the two frogs.

"Yes, and this whole formula you've been trying to come up with will not work. A formula will not give you any possibility for being responsible for the transformation in your life, will it?" Big Frog asked.

"No, I don't think so," I said, still amazed by my realization. "It's more like a way to avoid responsibility."

"And, if you can't keep transformation alive by your memory of it, how will you keep generating it in your life?" he asked.

"I don't know," I said. It seems like...well, I don't know."

"When you spoke of your family, were you present to the possibility you saw earlier?" Lady Frog asked.

"To some degree, I was. It seemed like when I told you about it, I became present to it for just a minute."

"Keep that before you. It will have significance for you in the future," Big Frog said. "That is all for now."

The frogs dismissed me to ponder the brief lesson. I rubbed my eyes and in an instant, both frogs were gone.

CHAPTER 15

Love and Reason and "By the Way"

Lady Frog sat before me as I awoke from a meditation in which I had fallen asleep. I was seated beneath the old cypress, still posed for meditation. My body had a light covering of wetness from the mist of the nearby falls.

She was poised on a broad leaf positioned at my eye level. The sun reflected brightly off her moist, lime-green body, catching my sleepy eyes and causing me to squint involuntarily.

I'd been dreaming, though I couldn't recall clearly any of the details of the dream. It seemed that it had something to do with the subject of love. I awoke with some discomfort concerning the matter.

Lady frog understood my confusion, as she usually did. She abruptly began communicating with me.

"Are you aware of when you have fallen in love?"

Surprised by the question, I looked at her.

"Well, I suppose it was when I met my wife," I replied.

"Oh, that is not the truth," she told me, as she shifted on her platform, causing the leaf to bounce violently.

Her instability made me think she might fall off. I couldn't see any way that she had gotten onto that leaf in the first place.

"Are you all right?" I asked.

She ignored my concern.

"You may have fallen in love with your wife, and indeed you may love her. They are not the same, and you have fallen in love before and since then," she said.

I reached into the pond with both hands and splashed cold water onto my face. The shock caused my body to shiver.

"I know this has something to do with the confusion I awoke with," I said back to her. "And, I think I'm even more confused right now."

"Notice how confusion becomes your mind's ally when you are faced with the opportunity to transform that which has so identified you in your past," she said.

Though she was no longer moving, her energy seemed to be causing her leafy podium to bounce.

"What I wish to communicate to you," she said, "is that you have indeed experienced falling in love many times, even since you came to be in this place. You may even fall in love within the next few moments."

"Please go on," I begged, drying my face with the sleeves of my sweatshirt.

"Being in love is the most glorious and inspiring way of being that I know. Love is pure possibility. For me to experience being in love with you, all there is for me to do is to be present with you, allowing you to be who you are, exactly the way you are."

I had a sense of what she was saying, because in her presence I could feel her sincere love for me.

She continued, "I will say it this way. Being in love does not mean merely loving someone. Loving someone involves putting forth effort. It can and will devolve into reason. If you do something that touches or inspires me, I may love you because of it. If you do something I don't like I may stop loving you because of that."

"Is it possible," I asked, "to love someone for no reason?"

I was thinking about the words that had earlier come to me concerning choice.

"Oh yes," she answered, "It is possible to love without reason. In fact, love for another always begins without reason. It is the outcome of falling in love and has its existence inside the speaking of it. Humans do not always understand this. They tend to add their own interpretations of why they love someone or are loved by them. That has nothing to do with who a person is or any experience of love. Being in love is simply standing in the possibility that love is in relationship to another. The most intimate place to be, love is surrendering to being, thus 'falling' in love."

I moved closer to the frog, anticipating something great from her.

"For someone who does not grasp this, or who does not understand one who has mastered the concept, it is likely a difficult possibility for the mind to hold. However, when one is in love, expectation does not exist. Being right or judging the other as wrong does not occur, since righteousness is a different possibility of being, which cannot live in the same space with love. Love is pure expression of being present with another, in the moment…here and now."

Lady Frog's discourse had begun to have an hypnotic effect on me. I caught myself backing away, trying to maintain control, wanting to not be dominated by having to understand what she was saying.

"One may recall having been in love in the past. That is a memory of something. Being in love is always right now, not in our memories."

Lady Frog's podium had begun oscillating back and forth in a slow figure-eight movement.

"I love the experience of being in love," she continued. "It is the most empowering presence of all. When one defines 'being in love' differently, one may not see this the same way. It may be that one thinks of being in love as a necessarily romantic thing and attempts to create love in relationship by doing romantic things.

"One might also have an expectation of experiencing romance with another. One might believe that two beings in love are bound together, that no others can or should experience that same possibility of being with those so bound, that they are mates.

"Notions about love may be at the core of how one has identified oneself over a lifetime. Those notions are not the truth, though in one's reality they may seem like the truth. It is a possible way to be, perhaps a cultural paradigm that holds human beings, even when they do not know they are held by it.

"Love, or the lack of it, is a source of insecurity and the very place where human beings search for their security. Security does not manifest out of one's trying to love and certainly not by wanting love. You either love or you do not."

After a long, still, silent pause, I looked into Lady Frog's eyes. She was right. I had indeed fallen in love during our conversation.

For the first time, I noticed details about Lady Frog's appearance that I had never seen. Her skin had light green swirls and tiny black flecks. I saw her as a very beautiful frog. I was overwhelmed by her compassion. I suddenly became aware of many times during my lifetime when I had fallen in love. It was surprising to me how I had almost always operated under the notion that being in love had something to do with the idea of mating.

I recalled the utter strangeness that I always felt when it was suggested that one could be in love with someone outside of a committed relationship. Somehow, I had mentally combined the concept of being in love with the concept of being romantic, as if they were both the same thing.

"I again say thank you for having this conversation with me," I said to Lady Frog. "I am now quite aware of when I have fallen in love in my life."

"You are again welcome, and I love you too," she said, anticipating what I myself wished to say to her. There was a pause, and then she said, "And now, do you want to tell me what it is that you have been withholding?"

I took a step back. My bare foot landed on a sharp rock, causing a horrendous pain to shoot up my leg and into my back. I dropped to the ground and grasped my foot, massaging the afflicted spot.

"What I have been withholding?" I asked with a pained expression.

"Yes, the source of your confusion, which still resonates in your being."

"I thought we just had that conversation," I said, still rubbing and feeling sharp twinges in my foot.

"We had a conversation about falling in love. We did not have a conversation about the confusion from your dream."

"Oh…well, I'm not sure what that was anymore."

"Yes, and you continue to hide from your own inquiries."

"Well, I just didn't think it was important right now."

I wished she would ask me about the pain in my foot instead. I pressed my thumbs into the area where it hurt.

"What is it that you do not think is important?"

"The dream I had in my meditation," I confessed. "I was confused by it. I'm not even sure I can remember it clearly enough to talk much about it now."

"What do you remember about it?"

"I remember seeing Big Frog and you…" I hesitated. "You were together in the dream…copulating," I said, embarrassed.

I looked past Lady Frog to the pond, where a small blackish frog was just landing at the surface, having leaped from a rock and missed the lily pad it had apparently aimed for. I started to laugh.

"And you have some confusion about that?" she asked with no apparent embarrassment.

"Well, it wasn't just that. It was a pretty graphic dream, and it wasn't just your act of sex that got my attention. You appeared, in this dream, to be with each other in a way that made me think you were deeply in love; and yet I never had any sense that you were committed lovers in the way I would have expected."

"Yes, and what is your confusion about that?"

"That's what I don't understand. Frogs aren't humans. For humans, sex is usually considered an act of love. Being passionate with someone usually involves a desire to be together in a relationship. I don't know how that is for you."

"And that information is from your encyclopedia of humans?"

"Well, yeah…can you see my confusion now?"

"I can see you are confused. It is the place for us to inquire now."

"I was afraid you were going to say that. But, I don't even know how to start looking at this."

The pain in my foot subsided. I stopped massaging.

"A place to start is with your statement about humans and sexuality. Then we can go back to your dream if we need to."

"Okay, but I'll warn you, I'm not going to like this," I said. "As soon as I said humans have sex as an act of love, I knew I'd put my foot in it."

"You put your foot in it?"

"It's a human expression," I said.

"I'm not even sure I said it right. What I meant was that I put my foot in my mouth, meaning that I said something I knew was not right even as I was saying it. I know humans have sex very often when it has nothing to do with love. At least some do."

"And what does it mean if humans have sex when it's not for love?"

"I don't know. I suppose it doesn't mean anything."

"Yet, it is the source of your confusion."

"Mine and about a billion-and-a-half other people's."

"Ah, so there is something to inquire into here after all."

"Yeah, I guess so."

The beautiful Lady Frog had steered me into another place where my mind wanted to forbid me to look. I suddenly remembered an episode in my life from years earlier. I told Lady Frog about it.

"About two o'clock one morning, I woke up thinking about a woman. I was concerned about the way our last conversation had ended. I wished I'd been clear with her that I wasn't just looking to have a sexual relationship with her, that I wanted something more than that. I wanted her to know that I wanted a loving relationship with her.

"I had said something like that to her, but distinctly without the 'I am not looking to have sex with you' part. What a crock that was. I did just want to have sex with her, and I was doing everything I could to maneuver her into believing it was her idea so I wouldn't look like a jerk. I had wanted to have sex with her the first time we met, the very moment we met, if I could have worked it out.

"As I was laying there thinking about what I should have said to her, I started to realize how willing I was to say anything, to lie, in order to have sex with a woman. Why couldn't I just tell her what I wanted and let her decide if she wanted it too? No, she would never agree with such a straightforward approach. It was better to sell her on the idea first.

"I imagined she probably saw right through my crap the whole time and wanted no part of me. Maybe she was left with confusion about what I really wanted from her, the way I was confused.

"As that night wore on, I was in a quandary over my strategies. My mind stayed hard at work on the dilemma. I couldn't seem to get my emotions under control.

"I realized I was in the throws of something. I was trying to break through something regarding the whole idea of sexuality in my life. The problem was that I didn't know a thing about how to break through something that had me so confused."

"What were you afraid of that you could not tell her the truth about your desire for her?" Lady Frog asked.

"I'd been struggling the whole time I knew her," I replied. "At first I just wanted her for her looks. There was something about the way she carried herself, her presence. I didn't tell her then because I'd just met her and didn't think it was a socially appropriate thing to say.

"It was still that way the next few times we saw each other, but eventually there came a point in our relationship when I started to really like her and care about her. That was when I began to struggle with the question—if I do care so much about her, why am I so conscious of wanting to have sex with her? Why was I spending so much of the time fantasizing about her?

"I thought something must be wrong with the way I was thinking about it. I couldn't figure out what I wanted. I wasn't sure if I could be sincere to her. I doubted myself and felt guilty about it. I was afraid I might be faking my attention and support just to get closer so I could have sex with her. At the same time, I knew I really did care for her and wanted a relationship with her. But I really wanted to have sex with her.

"I imagined different ways of bringing up the question of sex. I avoided dealing with the possibility that our relationship might be in jeopardy, and still could never quite reconcile my fixation on sex.

"I knew other beautiful women, and didn't have that inability to be straight with them. I had no concern about letting them know if I had nasty thoughts about them. There were also women I didn't have sexual thoughts about and simply wanted friendship from.

"With this particular woman, I constantly struggled between having both sexual thoughts and caring thoughts. I tried to protect my image in her eyes, not wanting to lose her respect. All the while I suspected she must have picked up on my confusion, because it seemed to impact our time together sometimes."

I looked at Lady Frog wondering if I had put her to sleep. She was still with me.

"So you met a woman and had a sexual desire. You did not truthfully communicate your desire to her, and in the process of strategizing to create your opportunity, you developed an affinity. Your affinity for her then conflicted with your sexual intentions."

"Your version is a lot simpler than mine."

Saying all this to Lady Frog, I started to get the idea that I had caused myself to wake up in a conflict over my desire for the woman. For the first time, I actually saw how I had allowed it to go that way.

"I don't suppose it makes any difference for me to say what I have just realized about all that," I said, "but here it is. I think I've combined sex and love as though they're one single concept. The truth of the matter is that I wanted to have sex with her. I was sexually attracted to her. I've just realized that just as that droplet of water was only a droplet of water, sexual desire is sexual desire, and that's what it is. "I may truly have loved her, but I did want a sexual relationship with her.

"The other thing I see is that the way I was being about it was not as somebody who loved her. Truthfully, there was no way she would ever know I loved her while I was acting like that. When I said 'I love you' to her, she was undoubtedly hearing 'Let's have sex.' She might also have been hearing my trepidation, and who knows what effect that was having on her.

"It doesn't make any difference for that relationship, but now I think I'm clear about the two distinct concepts of love and sex. What that means is, I never really needed to justify my sexual desire by making myself believe that I loved her.

Loving her was simply empowering her, and allowing her to be herself. Wanting sex was just the man that I was being attracted to the woman she was."

"What do you think might have made a difference to how you both experienced all of that?" Lady Frog asked, now sitting perfectly still on her leafy platform.

"I think there are two things I can see that might have made a difference. One would have been knowing that I was combining the concepts of love and sex. That might have allowed me to separate the two concepts while the whole thing was going on. The other thing could have been, once we knew each other well enough, being straight about what we really wanted from each other. I could have been honest about suggesting we consider a sexual relationship. It would have been her option to say yes or no, to make a different suggestion, or even to be offended by my suggestion. I might have accepted any of those responses and been able to deal with them.

"The breakthrough for me, I suppose, would have been simply letting her know that she was free to respond any way she wanted to for her own reasons. Saying yes could have meant having sex because we wanted it, not because we loved each other. Saying no could have meant not having sex because we didn't both want to, not because we didn't love each other. For all I know she might have wanted to have sex, but was put off by me acting like I was in love with her."

"And what else might have been different for you?"

"For myself, I could have known that she was there for me because she wanted to be, and it was up to me to allow her to be who she was about that. I was already part of her life regardless of what I said or what I wanted. At the same time, I know I wanted to have dirty sex with her, and I wanted her to want that, too. She might not have, and I probably would have been disappointed about it, but it wouldn't have had the same impact had I not combined the concepts of love and sex. I think that was where I killed off the whole relationship."

Lady Frog listened to my account. I could tell she understood and knew I wasn't really speaking of only that one occurrence in my life.

Maybe the whole thing started for me in fifth grade when a girl I really liked asked me to give something to her and said, "I won't love you any more if you don't."

On the other hand, maybe it was in seventh grade gym class when a certain pretty and very nasty girl, who I found very attractive, said in front of a group of girls, "I'm going to pull down your pants to see if you have any pubic hair yet."

I can't say which of those two incidents was scarier for me. Certainly, by the time I graduated from high school, I had a full-on dichotomous relationship between being straight about love and sex and protecting myself to the point of never fully going for what I wanted, love or sex, in any relationship with any woman.

"I suspect," Lady Frog said, "that neither love nor sex occurred after that time in your relationship with her, did it?"

"No, and I suppose that was the price of my confusion. She didn't wait around for me to figure out what I wanted. And, that wasn't the first, nor was it the last time my failure to distinguish love from sex cost me a relationship."

Lady Frog gazed at me in silence, making me think she was looking deep into my eyes for something.

"Is there anything else you want to say about that, or about your dream?" she asked.

"Well, I now see that the dream was probably the gateway to this conversation with you," I said. "Also, it's interesting to note that my relationship to love and sex was yet another place where I was dealing with my life as problems and solutions." I paused a moment, then said, "Until I was willing to acknowledge the truth about my ideas regarding love and sex, and to be responsible for who I was and who I am in the matter, I had almost no access to what could be possible regarding either aspect of my life."

I paused again, looking into Lady Frog's dark eyes.

"I just realized that the reason I am here with you is because I couldn't be straight with my wife about what I wanted. She kept asking, but I just couldn't say."

Lady Frog seemed to smile. She didn't say anything.

"I really want to thank you for the love and support you have given me since I have been here," I said. "I do truly love you."

"You are very welcome," she said. "And I thank you for this moment, and your willingness to stand in the face of your own resistance. You inspire us all. We all know your love and extend you ours forever."

"Wow…and wow! When I sat down, I thought I was just going to sit here and meditate for a while. Wow!"

I couldn't say anything more. I stood and bowed to Lady Frog, and we both went our own way.

CHAPTER 16

The Inequality of Humans

One early evening, I had hiked up the path beyond the falls. I was strolling along in the high meadow, enjoying the furry softness of the tall foxtail grass gliding under my hands, when a thought came to me.

By now, I was quite used to the way lessons began as either a thought or a voice in my head. What surprised me this time was that this particular thought I was having seemed out of place in the gorge. I couldn't imagine it would ever be a consideration for the frogs.

"Why do you not think we would be aware of that which so plagues the world you live in, human?"

I was struck by the question. I started to wonder if it was my own thought that caused the question, or the question that caused my thought. I couldn't tell who was communicating with me.

"I uh…"

I had no answer. I looked around, curious to see who had spoken to me. The meadow was empty and quiet. A slight breeze caused a ripple on the pond-like surface of the grass.

"You brought this inquiry into being," I heard addressed to me. "It was for this purpose that we have met in this place."

"Who are you? When did we meet?" I asked, puzzled.

I waited for a reply but there was only silence.

"Hello?"

No reply. The meadow was suddenly very still.

I kept thinking about the strange communication. Unable to understand why the conversation had abruptly stopped, I tried to ask Big Frog, but there was no reply from him. In fact, none of the frogs were responding to any of my questions.

Suddenly, I felt alone and rejected, disappointed, upset. I sat down in the tall grass. My mind began to fill with thoughts about what was happening. I looked around and wondered what I had done wrong. I decided to try thinking back to the mysterious conversation.

I spoke aloud, "There was a question about that which plagues the world I live in. What was that about? I brought the inquiry into being? What does that mean?"

My thinking seemed to get me nowhere. I was aggravated and upset about the frogs seemingly abandoning me. I tossed my head back and put my hands over my eyes, drawing in a deep breath of the fresh mountain air. I held it, listening to the stillness.

"I have to clear my mind," I thought to myself.

At that particular moment, my mind was anything but clear. I started to consider the things I thought I could be certain of, again speaking aloud.

"Okay, so I had a conversation with someone I didn't recognize. Did he find it offensive that I didn't recognize him? Is that why no one will communicate with me now?"

I thought at first that this could be it, but then abruptly rejected the notion.

"No, I've been much more offensive than that since I've been here. None of you get offended that way. It must be something else.

"I brought the inquiry into being. How did I do that? What was I doing?"

A moment later, I started to recall in detail what had actually happened. I had been walking in the meadow. A certain thought had occurred to me.

I remembered thinking it strange to have that thought here, and that was when the question was asked. I had assumed the particular thought related only to the world of humans, specifically regarding the intolerance we humans have for each other.

It was a thought about the insidiously foul way we humans treat each other. It was about how human beings prevail over each other, about the inequality of humans, how we humans behave unjustly toward anyone who acts in any way different or outside of our normal social order. It was a thought about cultural, racial, sexual, religious, financial, and social inequality among the tribes of humanity.

"Yes, and why do you not think we would be aware of that which so plagues the world you live in?" The question suddenly reverberated.

"I just didn't think it would be something that would be considered here," I replied into thin air.

"And, you think that what is considered here are questions about whether you recognize who you are communicating with?"

"I suppose I was stunned by the question you asked me," I said.

Something about the voice started to seem familiar.

"Human, you dwell among us. You are indeed quite different from us, in case you think that does not get noticed."

"I'm certain that it does," I replied. "But, I've not felt any intolerance or hatred from any frogs while I've been here."

"What is this hatred that you speak of?"

"Oh, so you're going to ask me the tough questions right away?" I asked, attempting humor. "I'll have to think about that."

"What is hatred? What do you consider to be the source of it? From what place does human hatred spring?"

"Well, in a quick answer, it seems to me that one source of hatred has its roots inside of intolerance. Intolerance for being different than what is expected, not fitting in with a particular order. Other sources might have something to do with greed or jealousy, like wanting to take something that someone else has."

"What is there about being different that would produce this intolerance that you speak of?" he asked, but then suddenly interrupted my response. "Ah, wonderful! You are becoming present, human."

He was referring to my beginning to seek a relationship with him, rather than concerning myself with his identity. I not only was having the conversation, I was actively engaged in looking with my mind to see him, to be with him, to engage him in this inquiry in the most powerful way possible.

No doubt, he was already that engaged with me. I could feel his presence, though I still was not able to see him. I chose to deal with him as he presented himself.

"What is there about being different?" I repeated the question. "It seems most likely that fear drives our intolerance," I stated, trying to sound as though I knew what I was talking about.

"Fear?"

"Yeah, fear," I said.

I knew I was stating the obvious, but I needed to begin saying something, anything. I needed to start from someplace.

"I don't know where the fear originates from—maybe from some perceived threat to whatever is already in place, what is familiar. It seems that people who are in control very often engage in quashing anyone who is different and who might challenge their position, the current reality, so to speak."

"People who might challenge their position? That is interesting. Explain what you mean when you say humans fear those who might challenge their position. Say more about what you mean when you speak of being different."

"I'll try to relate it this way," I said. "When I think about what I have learned about the history of the United States, the country where I am from, I'm sometimes faced with injustices that befell groups of people who were important to the development of our country into the nation it became. Some were the human beings who inhabited North America before the Europeans discovered and invaded the New World. Those original people were conquered, robbed of their homelands, and in many cases killed or incarcerated as whole populations. Those who were 'willing' among them were assimilated into the prevailing Euro-American society that overtook the land.

"There was also the African slave trade. Again, through some judgment of superiority, Euro-Americans dominated and destroyed whole cultures from Africa. They believed they could own other humans like property, and considered African-American people as subhuman for centuries in America.

"Chinese people were imported into the country like livestock as cheap and expendable labor for such dangerous and unappreciated work as the building of America's Transcontinental Railroad.

"Dustbowl farmers of America's heartland were displaced by their own poverty and by scheming politics. The great machine of corporate power surreptitiously enslaved them.

"Migrant workers from Mexico, willing to endure societal indecency in the hope of finding their way out of poverty, were trapped into that same inhumanity to humanity so that American companies could benefit from their cheap labor.

"During our Second World War, Americans of Japanese descent were herded into concentration camps by a 'representative' government that said its aim was to protect them from a suspicious American society.

"And the American government was also complicit in the domination of men over women, who were historically thought of and treated as inferior beings, suppressed, not allowed to vote, prevented from competing for work, and made subservient.

"It seems that these episodes in American history display not only greed, but a propensity toward dominating any cultural rise that could conflict with the established order.

"The arrogance of America has bred a complex and dangerously divided landscape of fear and hatred that cries out for solace and simultaneously suppresses itself in its own despair. And here I am, as American as any other, wishing I didn't have to account for any of my own thoughts, dominating the entire world with my derisive thinking, avoiding responsibility for being who I have been in that world.

"Acts of intolerance have been perpetrated against virtually every culture that dared to display the pride of its own identity in difference to the Euro-American ideal. These were acts of arrogance originating out of a desire to hold power, perhaps even with an undercurrent of societal domination. What has happened in America and around the world has been the genocidal annihilation of the cultural identity of entire human populations.

"The very humanness of a culture can likely call forth its own resistance, even when that very resistance might bring on eventual destruction of that which it so eagerly defends."

A wind stirred, causing a gentle wave across the meadow at first, and then whipped violently as I passionately voiced my thoughts.

"Over time, as the societal notion of superiority has become known to be false, it has been replaced by outright fear, maybe fear of admitting the truth about what we humans have done to each other. The newest threat isn't necessarily cultural—it is the threat of being dominated by our own truth. This failure to be, along with the powerful resistance of persecuted people, possibly affects the entire American society. Assimilation, although it may have been intended to yield a homogenous society, is not currently possible because we Americans can't stand in the presence of our own culture that so represents a past we cannot ourselves reconcile.

"The truth is, I can't even begin to say what I think is behind why humans destine to prevail over each other. White Americans, Black Americans, Native Americans, Hispanic Americans, Asian Americans, Arab Americans, Jewish Americans all seem to be at the mercy of their fear and are to some level suspicious and hateful toward each other. I even think, to some degree, we are hateful toward ourselves.

"Part of it might be the desire to remain pure in our cultural paradigms. What was it about Hitler's sadistic obsession that could have driven a whole intelligent nation to attempt the eradication of an entire race of people inside and outside its borders?

"As a people, humans want to exclude challengers from ever having any opportunity to destroy our own cultural identity. We maintain righteousness about that which we identify as being ourselves. We condemn others for the identity that we ourselves saddle them with through our judgments about them. From that position, there can be no possibility for any race or culture to exist alongside any other over time. There is only the righteous position that grips us all.

"The idea gets even more insidious as our notions of cultural survival play out inside our cities, our neighborhoods, our families—between brothers and sisters, husbands and wives, children and their own parents.

"Human beings kill each other regularly in order to assure the survival of what we think is the truth. Right is right, and murder, even mass murder, becomes justified in the minds of those who commit such atrocities.

"It may be simple fear of change that drives our behaviors. Humans are gripped by the illusion that we know who we are and that we actually have what we think is ours—family, property, country, our thoughts. We will not give up our comfort of knowing and controlling, regardless of the consequences.

"As individuals, we are identified by our pasts, which we believe to be who we are. We're comfortable with our identity. It's so pervasive among us that we invite others to participate in our communities if they share a similar past. Our communities become extensions of our individual ideologies, becoming a singular identity at a community level. We then have the comfort of being recognized in a culture with a particular consensus.

"When anyone, or anything, not recognized by us challenges our position of certainty, our fear of change can take over our behavior. We must then change whatever dares to offend us into something recognizable before it has the opportunity to change us. We have a deathly fear of losing our identity.

"What's different about people is our perceived human identity. Challenge a person's identity and you will be hated. Challenge the identity of a culture, and someone is sure to die."

"And so," said the frog after a pause, "it is this fear of losing one's identity that causes humans to differentiate themselves from others and perhaps perpetrate these negative behaviors against them?"

"But the fear is not simply a fear of those other humans. It is their disagreeable or unrecognizable ideas that are feared by us. We can't stand in the face of not recognizing without somehow trying to kill the offending idea. It seems to be an automatic reaction of human beings. Somehow, at the source of it, may be this whole history of human emergence having to do with language and communication and world domination."

"Thus, the discrimination comes full circle."

"Yes. The entire world is divided into camps. There are those who perceive themselves as being alike. There are those who are perceived as different. There are even those who don't fit either category. They are perhaps the ones who occur as being most different of all, appearing to fit the culture, yet by some disagreeable assertion, not empowering the 'alike' category in its dominance over the 'different' camp.

"People who don't go along with dominance are called 'sympathizers.' They weaken consensus. They might be the biggest challenge of all to a culture's identity and are hated possibly more than the really different people."

As I spoke, I lost myself in the discourse. Maybe it was my identity that disappeared, if only for those few moments. I became aware that I had myself been face-to-face with something unidentifiable the whole time. It was then that I suddenly saw the humor of my own recognizable identity. The wind that had been so violent quickly diminished to a yielding breeze. I realized that I had been talking about myself, about my own human identity, and about my own humanity.

In that moment also, I saw a glimpse of the frog with which I had been communicating. It was none other than the mysterious little frog that I had suspected of following me and playing an awkward game with me during the earliest days of my arrival. It was the frog that would never communicate with me. The frog was clumsily positioned somewhere in a dark dry spot under a pile of rocks.

I suddenly understood why we had not communicated until now. We couldn't. There was no communication for us to have. It was this conversation that was the purpose of our meeting. I wasn't ready for it until now. I was not able to deal with his being different.

"Perhaps now you may see, my friend, the level of your preparation for the Great Meeting?" Big Frog interjected, as he joined our conversation in the meadow, suddenly appearing just a few feet away from me in a depression in the grass.

"Say a little more about that," I urged.

"We promised you, in the beginning, that you would be prepared. We have taken you through situations which have caused this to happen. Today, your twenty-second with us, you have become the trainer, distinguishing for us a context for existence that pervades your own humanity, the context of fear for survival. I declare that you are ready for your Great Meeting."

CHAPTER 17

Forgiving

The dotted line of the stream far below connected the green oak and cypress canopy sprawled above the narrow valley floor. From the perspective at the top of the waterfall, the ancient and giant cypress tree appeared isolated and minuscule in its lonely station next to the falls and against the gray rock face of the gorge.

I sat half-mesmerized by my inspirational view of the hidden ravine. It was the last evening before my Great Meeting.

"When you forgive someone, what you are restoring is the integrity of your own self," the ancient frog said in a pleasant voice that seemed grandfatherly to me.

The comment might have disappeared into the forever unheard had my consciousness not snatched it out of the air just as it was escaping to oblivion.

Taking a moment to consider the statement, I replied, "That is an interesting thing you said. I wouldn't necessarily have thought of it is as my integrity being restored, but rather the forgiven person's."

"Yes, I can see how it might look that way to you," the elder frog said. "Let's have a conversation about it so we may see if you are right."

He moved deliberately and slowly into a shallow, water-filled rock impression supplied by water splashing continuously over from the stream that was itself destined for the long drop of the falls. I felt a momentary shudder of fear that the old one might get too close and be swept over in the torrent.

"Well, by now, I'm clear that every conversation I have before the Great Meeting is an inquiry and a lesson, not to mention a roller coaster ride for me,"

I said jokingly, as I positioned myself to pluck the old frog up to safety, if necessary.

"I don't know what a roller coaster ride is, but I can tell you are speaking of the tide of emotions you experience when you inquire into something important about your own life."

"Yes, to put it mildly," I said. "What question do you have for me?"

"First of all, for what reason would you ever need to forgive someone else?"

"I expect it would be because that person said or did something that made me upset," I said.

"So," he said, almost before I finished speaking. "When someone says or does something that impacts your emotional state?"

A large splash of water suddenly washed him closer to the stream's edge, startling me. I jumped, but not in the direction of saving the fragile old frog. Had it been a more powerful wash I would have watched stupefied as he disappeared to a certain death. I resolved to be more reactive.

"Well, yes," I replied.

My familiar confusion flared at the question.

"And by saying or doing whatever it was, that person's integrity is somehow impacted?"

"I believe so," I said with a tone of caution, and looking at him with a similar expression of carefulness. "Don't you think so?"

I held my gaze.

"Oh, young human," he said. "What I think is of no consequence here. The question is about the integrity of one's self."

"When you say 'the integrity of one's self,' are you talking about one's sense of wholeness?" I asked, thinking I already knew something and trying not to look arrogant, as if the way I looked would be how he would know.

"Yes," he said.

I stuttered, hoping for a bit more elaboration.

I asked, "Well…how is it that another person who says or does something can impact my integrity?"

I really was confused and, this time, quite certain of my justification for it. As happened often in the gorge, I was now being forced to look deeper than the initial consideration would likely have taken me.

"Okay," I said. "I'd better stop messing around here and start engaging."

"A splendid idea," the amicable old frog said.

He looked into my eyes, giving me the familiar sense that he was checking to see if I was ready to continue.

"What happens when someone says or does something and you become upset?"

"Well…hmmm."

I paused to consider the question. At the same time I was wondering how old this grandfatherly frog might be if he was calling me a young human.

"Okay, let me try this. They say or do whatever it is, and my reaction is to get upset."

"And, what about what they say or do makes you upset?"

"My first answer would have been that it was what they said or did that made me upset, but I already know that is not what you're asking. So, let me see…what makes me upset is…probably…my reaction to what they said or did."

"Okay, and you have already said that. Now tell me, what is the impact their action has on you that makes you react by getting upset?"

The old frog seemed unaffected by another sudden large volume of water sweeping him up onto the edge of the rushing creek. He simply pushed himself back down in the puddle and continued to look at me.

"Well, there is always some judgment that I make about what is said or done. They say or do something. I react by judging it right or wrong. If I judge it wrong, I might get upset."

"And," the old frog said. "When you judge it right or wrong, what else is happening?"

"Well, I am making them wrong," I replied, already knowing what was next, and bracing for him to tell me.

"And, when you make someone wrong for what they said or did, what happens to your integrity?"

"Yes, I know…my integrity suffers because I am left with an upset, which leaves me less than whole."

"Then, you may now see that restoring your integrity is your own responsibility, and not that of someone else?"

"Unfortunately, I do see that," I said disappointedly. "And I can also see that in the act of forgiving that person, I can restore my own integrity. I can restore my self."

I moved a little closer to the elderly coach. I liked him and wanted to protect him, and I was now certain that my reactions might be too slow to catch him, given the attention I was placing on the conversation.

"And can that person's integrity suffer from the offending action?" he asked.

I nodded affirmative.

"Is there anything for you to do to restore that person's integrity?"

"I'm not sure if there is anything I could do that would restore someone else's integrity," I replied. "It seems like that would be that person's responsibility."

"Perhaps. Yet, communicating your forgiveness might make it possible for that person to restore his integrity. You might even ask the other to forgive you, though you may have no sense of having done anything to be forgiven for—although you did make that person wrong."

"Yes, I can see that," I said, leaning toward him with my hand poised as he sloshed toward the edge again.

"What else do you see about the relationship between forgiving another and restoring integrity?"

The elder frog was taking the inquiry to another level.

"Well, I'm not sure," I said. "I may have to think about it."

"Yes, and that may be the exact place to look for this inquiry."

The old frog began to take on that riddling quality I knew so well from my conversations with Big Frog.

"What do you mean?" I asked, though I now had another question in my mind concerning the old frog's relationship with Big Frog. "Are you referring to my thinking?" I added.

"Perhaps forgiving people for what they say or do is not all there is to look at in this inquiry," the old frog said.

"Okay, now I am beginning to see something here. I know there are times when I might make someone wrong for what they say or do. I think there might also be times when I make them wrong for simply how I think they're being," I said.

"Please explain what you mean by 'making someone wrong for how you think they're being,'" he said.

"Well, it might just be that I judge people regardless of what they say or do. Maybe even for the way they look or sound or smell—"

"Aha!" The old frog exclaimed. "You are beginning to see that your integrity can be impacted in many ways."

He pulled himself back down to the center of the little pool just as another splash came over the top of him. The water did not move him this time.

"Yes, and it's starting to become a pretty big insight," I said. "I was speaking about making others wrong, but it really involves any kind of judgment that I make about others, not just right or wrong. I judge them for being different, as I spoke of in the meadow today when I talked about how humans discriminate against those who are different. I judge others and then suffer for my own judgment. I have to be right about it. It drives a wedge between myself and others."

"And maybe between yourself and yourself," Old Frog said. "Can you forgive others for whatever you have judged them for?" he asked.

"I don't know. That seems pretty noble. I don't know if I could be that magnanimous."

Another large volume of water washed over the elder, but he was rooted.

"What is something you have judged someone for recently?" the old frog asked.

"Well…I judged you for being old."

"Yes," he said with a pleasant laugh of wisdom, "and how has that impacted your integrity?"

"Well, I've had difficulty being completely present with you. There is that little bit of thought that just hangs around in the space between us. Since we've been here I've been worrying about your safety, and whether I might need to protect you from being swept over the waterfall."

"I see," he said. "And is it possible for you to forgive me for being old?" He asked, looking directly into my eyes.

"Well, I think I can. But, I'm not sure."

"Give it a try."

"Okay," I said. "I forgive you for being old."

"Thank you," he said with surprising sincerity. "And what did that make available for you?" The old frog asked.

"Wow! You just became who you are and not the old frog."

"Yes, well, can you forgive me for being a frog?"

His voice in my head took on a new youthful quality.

"I forgive you for being a frog," I said with a laugh.

"And can you forgive yourself for being human?"

"I do forgive myself for being human."

My body began to feel that euphoric feeling of spaciousness. Suddenly, I was aware of the possibility of being in relationship at a level I'd never experienced before with anyone.

My companion in the inquiry asked me to simply be with the possibility for a while and see what I might see. He hopped away, disappearing under the bushes that lined the bank of the stream that flowed over the falls.

I sat there a few moments looking down into the darkening gorge. I started noticing insights coming up from the depths of my consciousness, as though my mind were still engaged in the conversation.

I recalled once reading about a man who competed in marathon races while pushing his son along in front of him in a wheelchair. The family's doctors had advised the man and his wife to place their child into an institution after he was born with a challenging disability. The experts thought it was the best way to avoid heartbreak for the family.

I was deeply moved and inspired by the amazing story of what this father did, and by the remarkable expression of courage it was for both the father and the son to go far beyond what anyone would ever expect from either of them under the circumstances.

It was not until this conversation with the elderly frog that I realized why I had been so touched by that story.

What this father had done was to forgive his son. He had forgiven him for not being healthy, for not being normal, for not being like him as a father desires and expects his children to be.

I realized that this wise father had summoned his heart and forgiven his son for being afflicted with a disease. This father had forgiven his son. More than that, he had also forgiven himself for his own self-judgment and guilt for allowing his son to be born with the disability in the first place. This man had integrity like no person I had ever known.

Seeing this, seeing the simplicity of it, I began to think about my own children. I thought about judgments I had been holding onto about them, about times when they had not called me on Father's Day or on my birthdays. I forgave them. I also forgave myself for the times when, due to my own corruptive reasoning, I had not called them on their special days.

What a gift it was to forgive my children, the people I loved so much, and to forgive myself. My integrity indeed became whole in that moment.

I suddenly felt a rush of vitality in my body that had not been there for a long time. I was able to let go of judgments I had been holding on to about myself and about my family. I looked forward to telling my wife and family that I forgive them, and asking them to forgive me.

Something else began taking shape in my thinking. I thought about the news of the day, each day in the normal human world, consumed by war or negotiations for peace—Asia, The Middle East, Eastern Europe, America, deeply troubled places in the world.

The pull of conflict always seems to be toward one position or another. It's a very difficult thing to remain neutral about any conflict. Even the idea of neutrality seems in some way to be taking a position that makes both sides wrong and thus siding against both. How neutral is that?

What started to manifest in my thinking was now a completely different way of relating to conflict in which each side must be neither right nor wrong.

My view began to shift, and I began to believe that there was no such thing as position. Then I realized that maybe there was even no such thing as conflict either.

"How can that be? This thought I am having. There are no sides in a conflict?" I asked Big Frog as he unexpectedly but again not surprisingly hopped out of the brush in the exact place where the old frog had earlier disappeared.

"Ah, yes," he answered. "How can there be no conflict when there are clearly opposing views?"

"That is the question," I said, somewhat befuddled. "I mean, whether or not I myself take a position, there are real conflicts that can and do occur in a diverse world, at least in the diverse human world I live in."

"And you make the assumption that the human world is a different world than that of the rest of creation?"

Big Frog plopped down in the same wet impression the old frog had left a few moments earlier. I had no fear for Big Frog's safety.

"Well, I suppose I am referring to the world of human beings," I said. "Whether or not it is the truth, it is real for human beings, isn't it?"

"Perhaps. And, given that reality which occurs in the minds of humans, or even in the collective mind of humanity, may not be inherently true or even born of truth, one might make the case that the idea of conflict is itself a product of that very occurring, a product of a concept we might call conformance."

"Yes, I see. In a world governed by conformance, opposition would not be tolerated, which then gives rise to the possibility of conflict."

"Very good!" Big Frog said, excited that I was now engaging in conversational inquiry without being led. "So, in a world governed by conformance, where opposition gives rise to conflict, the mere suggestion of breaking with the established agreement creates the opportunity to either establish a new order of conformance or to stand outside of agreement and in opposition to it."

"And," I continued, "not only the opportunity, but an expectation that each and every participant will, without fail, either position themselves at some level of alignment with one of the established points of view, or at some level of opposition to any established point of view, thus establishing yet another point of view."

I could feel Big Frog mulling over the possibility that we had begun to uncover in the inquiry. I was at once amazed at the speed with which I had become present to possibility, and at the same time filled with excitement to explore it further. I forged ahead.

"And in a world where everyone must be recognized to be at some level of opposition, there can be no possibility of not opposition or of wholeness. That is conflict."

"Yes!"

Big Frog was excited with anticipation; I had not seen him this way before.

"And you can see that what is automatically sacrificed in that world is the possibility of integrity," he said. "There can be no integrity in a world that rises to conflict."

I had not yet looked at it in those terms, but it suddenly dawned on me that integrity was indeed sacrificed. The world could not have integrity and wholeness in any conflict. Conflict is itself separation.

I began to see that the whole foundation for negotiated peace, such as between warring factions, is based on the idea that there really are opposing sides of a conflict.

People who are in conflict but wish peace must somehow hammer out an agreement that would then allow for an agreed upon peace.

I could also see that a peace arrived at under such circumstances might be tenuous and uncertain, and might even eventually fail. I tried to think of a single nation of human beings that I would call truly peaceful. I thought about incidents of suicide bombings and other forms of civil disobedience around the world and started to question whether so-called peaceful nations that were once comprised of separate, warring factions actually had become peaceful. Perhaps those with the dominant position had simply suppressed the less-powerful factions…the more successful the suppression, the more the appearance of peace. Maybe the cost of expressing a position had become too great, and factions had suppressed themselves in order to survive.

I recalled times during my childhood when I had been parentally forced to share something that was of value to me, something that belonged to me, with my undeserving brothers. Their ideal was that brothers should share, but I always had the feeling that in order to be considered a good person I was expected to give something of myself up.

There were times, in order to gain control, I underhandedly found a way to lose a contended item, and then viciously accused someone else of taking it to throw suspicion from me. Then I could have it all to myself again—even if only in secret.

"Ah, and thus we are returned to the original conversation from the day you arrived here," Big Frog said.

"What do you mean?" I asked.

"On the day we met, I spoke to you of the experiment and of the separation that came about as a result of human secrecy."

Shocked at the simplicity and the horror of what the frog suddenly made me aware of, I said, "It's as though I was an evil person, yet I never felt that way until just this moment."

"That you might feel that way now is understandable, given what you have become aware of in your time here. Remember though, it is still your humanity that causes you to interpret what you have seen as evil. Perhaps you may now understand how it is that you are in this place with us embarking on an adventure exceeding the limits of what has been possible in the world of human beings."

"I thought I was already having an adventure for the last twenty-two days."

"Recall that we discussed your preparation," he said.

"You mean I've just been packing for the trip, huh?"

"Perhaps. Or, maybe unpacking would be a more appropriate comparison."

I laughed aloud. I thought about the world I had left just a few short weeks ago, the failed attempts at peace negotiations in the Middle East, terrorist violence, impending war, death, the threat to the future of the world, the weak economy, the price of gasoline, market manipulation.

"What a mess," I said in my loud human voice as a tear began to form in my eye.

I looked at Big Frog and saw a shimmering of sadness in his eyes, perhaps a reflection of my own.

"You should rest," he said. "The Great Meeting is upon you."

My thoughts went to the Great Meeting. I was suddenly aware of the importance of the world being whole. My sadness gave way to a feeling that something had suddenly gone missing, and I stood there filled with a wanting for peace.

In that moment, I knew it was this visceral wanting that had been there for these frogs over the millennia since their realization that the world had become a dangerous place of separation. I suddenly knew I was in love with these frogs.

I stood silent for a long time, with not one occurring thought. My mind was truly silent.

Later, returning to the place where I had been sleeping for the last twenty-two nights, I sat for a while reflecting on my visit with the frogs. There was nothing else for me to think about. I was awake to possibility.

I lay myself down and saw the evening sky turn black in an instant, and fell asleep before my mind could register the sight of the stars above me.

CHAPTER 18

The Great Meeting

A single ray of sunlight shining through a minuscule crack in the high east wall of the gorge struck me in the face. It was as though a child were focusing a spot from a magnifying glass. I awoke, lethargic, and put my hand up to my cheek where the sun had created a hot spot.

I winced as my hand rubbed across the right side of my chin. It stung like the night of the accident at the stop sign. It seemed such a long time ago.

It was late in the morning. I lay there on my rock bed several more minutes, squinting, vaguely remembering another morning long ago, when I was a boy.

*   *   *

By 11:30 AM it was too late in the day for good fishing, not to mention that this water hole we had found, for all its natural beauty, seemed inhabited only by a lot of noisy frogs. Still, it was surprising the day had not yet progressed past the morning. It seemed to our small band of anglers that we had already been out all day.

They called me Teddy back then. I was a skinny, dark-haired boy—shirtless, tanned, and always caked with dirt from my head to the toes of my crusted and usually bare feet.

I stood on the steep and narrow path about thirty paces behind my father and brother, who both had already descended most of the way back to the floor of the gorge we had been exploring.

My father wasn't particularly concerned about the safety of his eight-year-old son. The path was not a treacherous one, no more so than most we used to tread in those familiar hills on our frequent quests for good fishing spots.

I lingered a few extra moments as I whispered to the stuffed frog I carried with me.

The bright green cloth frog of cartoonish appearance had been my constant companion longer than I could remember, and I was always able to remember a lot from very early on in my young life.

I remembered the Frosty Root Beers in the short fat bottles I so loved to get. They cost two dimes in the "lift-the-lid and slide-the-bottle" machine at the second-hand store next door to our old house on Ventura Boulevard.

We moved from there to the house on Tyler in 1959. I was three when we lived on Ventura, but my memories of those early days were strong.

I remembered having to be lifted up in front of that pop machine by my dad or older brothers because I had to pull out my own bottle, after inserting my own dimes of course.

I liked having my own money. Dimes were my favorite coins because they were smaller than pennies and nickels and worth more. I liked finding dimes where people lost them.

Sometimes people would lose dimes and didn't seem to care. They almost never looked for them when they dropped them. I always did. They were like treasure.

I remembered our homemade teeter-totter in the front yard. One time John, my oldest brother, jumped off the roof of the second-hand store and launched Charlie, the next oldest of the five boys, into outer space.

We all thought that was such a funny memory, but no one could remember how Charlie had lived through that one—maybe that was a time he suffered one of his many childhood broken bones. He always seemed to have some body part in a cast.

My stuffed frog laughed with the rest of us that day.

I remembered the giant pecan tree that canopied our whole back yard, and the tiny tree frog I found in it once. I wanted to keep him as a pet, but Dad told me it was wild and had to be let go. I complained to Mom, but she told me to think about the frog's mother and asked me how I thought she'd feel if some-one took one of us kids from her.

I remembered the nice lady who lived in the tiny shack at the rear of our lot. Her silver Airstream was parked under a white lattice-covered carport with flowering vines that climbed thick up the sides and over the top. That was some nice shade in the hot San Joaquin Valley.

I had a vague memory of pecan chocolate chip cookies. That made sense with that big old pecan tree there.

I looked down at Dad and Ben.

"Wait for me, I'm coming," I yelled out, running to the bottom of the path. "My shoes are over by the frog pond."

❀　　　❀　　　❀

I felt my cheek burning again from the spot of sunlight and came fully awake, realizing what day it was. It was the twenty-third day—the day of the Great Meeting! I looked at my watch and jumped up. I was excited.

The air was chill. I reached hastily for my gray sweatshirt lying on the ground. My flashlight fell out, striking the flat rock; the lens broke. I quickly picked it up, then paused a few thoughtful seconds looking at the shattered bulb inside.

I shoved the flashlight into my back pocket, put the sweatshirt on, and zipped it up three quarters of the way. I shivered a moment as my body adjusted to the shock of the cool material against it. I scanned from left to right, reading the newness of the morning. I felt an edge of excitement.

A large frog leaped into the pond with a resounding plunk. I watched the concentric circles spread across the surface as the creature disappeared into the dark water.

"Good morning," I said in the usual way of communication, waiting for the expectant reply.

There was none.

I started walking toward the falls, thinking the frogs would most likely be gathered there waiting for me, anxious to get started with our Great Meeting. I hoped they hadn't started without me.

I tripped over an unusual clump of grass along the edge of the pond.

Getting up quickly, I remarked to Big Frog, "Someone needs to cut this grass along here soon."

There was no reply from Big Frog. I began to feel a nauseating concern, but didn't know the source of it.

My thoughts were suddenly, "They've left me behind. I got up too late." Then I thought, "No, that's just me being lost at the fairground. They would have made sure I was up if it was time to go."

As I kept walking toward the falls, I noticed birds singing loudly, but stopping at my vulgar human approach. It suddenly dawned on me that I had never noticed any birds singing on any of the previous twenty-two mornings.

As a matter of fact, I didn't recall ever seeing or hearing any other animals except for the frogs—not even insects. I stopped walking and looked around carefully. Was I seeing this all for the first time?

A column of ants marched across a tree root and disappeared over the edge of a large rock. To my left, on the other side of the pond was the great huge cypress tree. That looked familiar, up against the shadowy gray sheer rock wall. I could see the falls ahead—yes, that too was familiar. Everything seemed to be in place, yet something was subtly different.

The flora seemed different, wilder, more full, and greener than each of the other days. There was not the multitude of colorful flowers I was used to seeing.

A cloud of mosquitoes hung in the shade of the trees by the water, seemingly waiting for me to come near so they could devour me. The grass was longer, not trodden, as was the path I was used to walking on. The mosquitoes followed me as I walked near the edge of the water, holding back, not willing to cross into the warm sunlit areas.

I arrived at the falls. All looked normal there, per my experience. The pathway I had often climbed to the meadow looked exactly as I thought it should. Everything seemed to be there, but much of the beauty that had for weeks so mesmerized me seemed to be missing.

I could find no meeting of the frogs. I was indeed alone. I calmed myself the way I had as a child at the county fair, telling myself I was not lost.

I sat down on the familiar rock ledge where I had meditated many times, my body starting to relax, wanting to go to sleep. I could feel myself back at the fairgrounds, ready to go find our old station wagon in the hospital parking lot.

"Wake up!"

Rubbing my fingers over a newly itching mosquito bite below my left ear, I looked at the pond very suspiciously, then at the cypress, and the wall of the gorge where I had witnessed the scene of the wonderful meeting. The sun highlighted the gray stone of the gorge wall—beautiful, but not picturesque.

At some point, sitting there, it hit me that I had just awakened from a dream. Though the gorge somehow was much as it had been inside my dream, it had to have been a dream—wasn't it?

There were no frogs to communicate with here. There was no Great Meeting. All that had seemed so real was no more than some manifestation that occurred in my sleep after I wandered into this lonely place seeking shelter the night before.

After sitting for what seemed like an hour, I dropped down from the ledge and continued my exploration, partly in the hope of finding that the dream really was true, and partly in amazement that a dream could so accurately depict an environment that was really there.

Leaving the dark cloud of hungry mosquitoes hovering in the shade, I walked up to the meadow—it was exactly as I had dreamed it. I lay myself down in the tall foxtail grass, feeling the breeze that caused the tops of the stems to sway like waves on a calm sea.

That dream was so real. I closed my eyes, hoping to recapture it, attempting to communicate with Lady Frog. There was no response from the frog I had fallen in love with—nothing. I got up and started back for the rock pathway, back toward the gorge.

There was a low humming sound in the distance. In a daze, I paused and looked in that direction. A moment later, a small airplane came into view. It flew in my direction and then veered off toward the higher peaks, disappearing into the morning sun on the other side of the forest beyond the meadow.

I heard the motor for a long while and then that too faded, leaving only the sounds of crickets, birds, and a small animal foraging under the tall grass a few feet away. I thought about Old Frog and Big Frog.

As I started back down the rocky path, I caught sight of something that appeared to be wedged in between some rocks just below me. When I got down to that level on the path, I bent down and reached in to try to grasp the object. My arm was not long enough. The item was in an awkward position.

I broke off a dry branch from a dead manzanita bush and got down on my hands and knees, poking around between the rocks. The thing I was interested in dislodged and fell toward me. I dragged it closer with the stick.

Just as I was about to reach in and grab it, I saw a glimpse of something moving in the rocks behind where I had been fidgeting. It was a snake. I couldn't tell what kind. It quickly disappeared back into the rocks below.

My heart turned over as I realized that I hadn't been paying attention to what I was doing.

"Of course there would be snakes," I said aloud. "I'm poking around in the rocks. This is Arizona. They have diamondbacks out here!"

I used the stick to pull the item out of the rocks where I could see it better. It turned out to be a little green stuffed frog. No doubt, some humans had been to this place before, and recently, judging from the apparent condition of the plaything.

I laughed to myself as I picked it up and turned it over, brushing the granite-sand and dust and pine needles off it. This stuffed frog looked remarkably like the strange frog I had been so enthralled by in my dream. It reminded me of something.

"No, that can't be," I thought.

Had I been receiving training from a stuffed frog? I put it in the pocket of my sweatshirt and continued my descent down the path, now wary of snakes and bears and mountain lions lurking behind every rock and shrub.

Back on the floor of the gorge, the mosquitoes must have tired of waiting for me to be their breakfast and moved off somewhere else. I looked around once more, gazing long at the silty pond. It was a curious feeling, having a dream so real, to actually stand in the setting where it had taken place.

Somehow, I knew that this dream was not about the place. I felt the stuffed frog in my pocket and wondered if I might still be dreaming, thinking to myself what a story this would make.

"Man dreams that he has a dream, and in the dream he awakes and…"

I began recalling other details of the long-ago morning as a child on the path. We had gotten up early and gone fishing.

We hadn't caught anything except for a few stupid bluegills, which I caught. I called them stupid because I sat on the bank and watched them commit suicide biting the hook with no bait on it. I just dangled it in front of them as I stood right there where they could see me, and they went for it like it was their last meal, and I jerked them out of the water. We'd be eating bony stupid bluegill that day, since we didn't catch any trout.

When Dad and Ben got tired of me catching stupid bluegill, Dad suggested we go for a drive and look for some new fishing spots.

We ended up exploring in a gorge. It was a lot like the one I was in now. I had my stuffed frog, which I had named Shadow because it was always with me. For some reason, I hid my frog among the rocks on the path, a path very similar to the one where I found this new frog.

Shadow had indeed been my very best childhood friend. I consulted with him about everything. Standing in the meadow that day with my dad and brother, Shadow had told me that I should hide him in the rocks and not to worry. I would see him again.

I remembered climbing down the path from the meadow and lagging behind Dad and Ben. I had stopped and put Shadow there in the rocks and told my dad that the frog had been lost. He searched the meadow and the path.

I remembered seeing Dad standing right over the rock hiding-place, looking down at the spot where I had put Shadow. He had to have seen him. Then it looked as though he were talking to someone as he stood there.

He suddenly came down the path and inexplicably said he couldn't find my frog. We went home, and though I missed Shadow for some time after that, I eventually stopped thinking about him.

"Though it is in their nature to be, not one of them dressed the part."

It suddenly came to me, the source of that curious phrase that I had heard in my mind on that first day exploring the gorge. It was something I had heard my dad say one day when I was playing with Shadow on our front porch. I never knew what he meant by it, though it probably made sense to him at the time.

My young mind thought that comment was so funny. It became my little joke with Shadow, and I said it to him often, posing him upright and dancing him around as I said it in my deepest little boy voice.

I chuckled to myself as I neared the place where I had spent the night on the rock, stepping over to the edge of the pond, gazing into the calm shallow pool where the pollywogs played in my dream.

The sun, shining through the trees, lit a small area. As I stood there, a group of pollywogs came into the lit area. Dropping to my knees, I rolled up my sweatshirt sleeve and reached into the pond, extending my index finger. A single tadpole swam curiously up to it.

Just as in my dream, when I began to move my finger toward the someday-frog, it darted away. And, just as in the dream, dozens of curious pollywogs began to play with my finger.

I smiled and said, "Well, at least I know you guys are real."

Lingering at the edge of the pond a few moments longer, I looked down and saw my own reflection looking back at me. In that moment, I recognized the person that I saw there, and I was calm.

I saw myself, perhaps for the very first time ever in my life. I saw myself not as the suffering soul who had left home on a quest to repair his broken life, but as a beautiful and whole human being. I saw myself as the droplet of water, as the possibility of possibility.

In that poignant moment of recognition, I truly forgave the self I saw looking back at me. Then I forgave all of humanity for everything that I had ever judged.

Pausing long, being with myself in the reflection, I asked, "Do you forgive me?"

I can't say that I heard an answer, but I knew somehow that I had been forgiven. For just a moment, I thought I saw my reflection as a little boy.

I smiled a satisfied smile and said to the reflection, "Hello, Teddy. I'm glad to meet you."

A moment later it occurred to me that I should be getting out of there and finding my way back to civilization, though after that dream, I wasn't certain why I should want to. I checked the area to make sure I was not leaving anything behind.

On the way back out through the crevice, I saw the place where I had hit my head coming in. The burned out flashlight bulb lay on the ground nearby. I picked it up and stuffed it in my pocket. In the light of day, I shuddered to see the number of places where I really could have split my head open running in the dark as I had.

From that point, I could see the refracted light, but not yet the opening where I had entered this world in the night. It did not seem quite so far in the daytime.

Near the opening, I saw the sky was clear. I was reassured that there was no fog. Stepping out cautiously, I was leery that the footing might be treacherous after the rush of water from the night before.

I was surprised to see that there was no mud. I scanned warily to be sure I hadn't come out a different place. Looking down, right at my feet, I saw the rope. It lay right where I had dropped it.

One hundred feet away, the car was in the exact spot where I had left it. There were a few puddles of water nearby, but no bog of mud, and no deep water. Off to my right I could see a signpost. From the back of it where I stood, I couldn't make out what the metal sign said.

I heard the sounds of the freeway, looked up to my right, and saw an eighteen-wheeler stopped with its windows fogged over. Every now and then, I could see the tops of other trucks passing by and I knew this truck was parked on the edge of the freeway.

Suddenly, there was a man walking around the truck. It was the driver stepping to the edge. He saw me and waved. I waved back.

I walked to my car. The door was ajar. The interior light was not on.

I thought, "Oh great, now the battery is probably dead."

I got in. The keys were in the ignition. I pressed the gas pedal down once, deliberately, and let up, slowly turning the key.

"Click," the engine roared.

"Sixty-two degrees here in Flagstaff this afternoon but it looks like a cold front is coming our way," the radio blared.

I clicked it off, swung out of the seat, and walked around the car. Untying the rope, I satisfied myself with the condition of the car. There was no scrape after all.

I read the road sign, "Freeway Entrance," with an arrow pointing the way to the on ramp. The entrance was just to the side of the granite rock face where I had run out of rope. Another few steps the night before and I would have known it was there. Of course, I would have missed the enlightenment of that wonderful dream.

I tossed the rope and my pack into the back seat as I got into the car. I had a feeling of lightness. Breathing the crisp air felt good. I put the car in gear and then drove onto the freeway entrance, where I stopped.

I rolled down the window and listened. There was the sound of the freeway. I could hear the car's motor humming with a slight squeak of the cold belts. In the distance, there was a sound like the bellowing of a bullfrog.

I smiled and said, "See ya," as I accelerated the car onto the freeway.

CHAPTER 19

Going Home

The next town to the east was Seligman. I pulled off the freeway and stopped at a gas station. After filling up the tank, I went inside to pay and asked the man if there was a good restaurant nearby.

"Don't know about good," he said, "but there's a place right up the road here. Ya go up here and take a left at Indian. It'll be right there on your right. You tell 'em I sent ya, and they'll give me a free breakfast in the mornin'."

"I'll tell 'em," I said with a smile. "You got a phone booth here?"

"What, you ain't got no cell phone, buddy? They just put in a brand spankin' new tower right there on the corner. Took 'em less than a week to construct the whole thing. I sat right here and watched 'em do it."

"Well, I bet you did. And I do have one, but I couldn't get a signal last night, and it doesn't seem to be working around here either."

"Drive right around to the other side of the buildin'," he said with a bow of his head and an exaggerated wave of his arm, as if he were dismissing me from his presence."

"Thanks."

I got back in the car and drove around to the phone.

"Hello?" I heard my wife's voice say.

"Hi."

"Well, mister. I was expecting to hear from you last night. I called your cell phone but it was out of range, or turned off. Are you okay?"

"Yeah, I got a little lost. I'm okay, and I'm in Seligman, Arizona. I'm going to get something to eat here and then get back on the road home."

"Home?" Her voice had a question and a concern. "I thought you were going to be gone three weeks."

"I was, but I want to come home now. I think I had a month's worth of vacation last night."

"Are you sure everything's okay?"

"Yes, I'm sure. Everything's perfect. I have a lot to tell you about."

"Not about any other women, I hope."

"Only one—with long, shapely legs."

"Mister, you'd better drive carefully. And, don't get lost any more, okay?"

"Okay, I will and I won't. I love you."

"I love you…bye."

"I really love you," I said to the dial tone before I realized she had already hung up.

I sat in the car for a long moment and thought about the dream. Even if it was only a dream, I learned a whole lot in one night. I felt different, but certain my life was changed forever.

I drove up to the restaurant. It would have been difficult to find if there had been any other buildings around. The only indication that it was a business was the yellow neon "OPEN" sign in the window of the yellow prefabricated building.

Looking through the window, I saw a man sitting on a stool reading a newspaper. He was lanky, with the same dark, sun-wrinkled skin as the man at the gas station.

"Hey, pardner," the man said, looking up as I walked in the door. "Can I help ya?"

He reached over the counter and turned down the talk radio station.

"O'Reilly," he said. "'No spin' he says. Danged guy's got more spin than an old ringer washin' machine."

"You're right about that," I said. "The guy down at the gas station told me about your place."

"That moocher. Ya know? He ain't paid for a breakfast in the nine years I worked here. He sends someone down here just about every day. Usually tells 'em the food is terrible, but it ain't."

"Well, I'm here and I'm hungry. What's your special?"

"Ya won't get any better frog legs than here, buddy. Stan and I—that's my brother down there at the fillin' station—go out giggin' two or three nights a week. Couple a years ago he up and tried to get married on me and we just about quit goin'. He found out she was seein' somebody else and called it off.

We got a special place we go. These are nice and fresh today, and some real big 'uns too."

"No, I don't think I'll have any frog legs today."

I had a brief thought about them gigging all the frogs in the gorge the night before.

"Do ya have a veggie burger on the menu?"

"No, we ain't got none of that veggie stuff around here. What, ya think you're still in California? You don't look like one of them California veggie men. Look like ya got some Okie in ya."

"Well, I do. My parents came out West back in the Grapes of Wrath days."

"Yeah, figgers. Ah well, how about a bean-and-cheese burrito? We don't use no lard or nothin'."

"That'll do. Thanks."

The frog king went over to the window and yelled to someone in the back. "Bean-and-cheese burrito platter, honey. No frogs for this guy."

"Okay, bean-and-cheese sans the frogs. You got it, baby." A pretty blonde with a Barbie-doll face looked out and made eye contact with me. I felt a flirtatious flash and smiled at her.

As horrible as frog legs sounded to me right then, I had to enjoy the decorum of this place. I looked above the counter at the chalkboard menu. The name of the restaurant, Jumper's, was at the top.

"Are you Jumper?" I asked. "Stan and you look a lot alike. I can tell you're brothers."

"Yup, that's my nickname. We're twins. Can ya believe that? He like ta never got over me takin' his fiancé away, but he finally forgive me. I don't know if I forgive him for stickin' me in the butt with that frog gig though. Had to get it cut out, and they give me a tetanus shot in the other cheek to boot."

"Couldn't sit down on that stool to do his paper readin' job for a week," Barbie yelled out of the back.

"Yeah, that's a couple brothers for you," I said. "Always fighting."

I thought to myself how appropriate it was that I came here.

I finished the bean-and-cheese sans the frogs and headed for the car. I heard the double jingle of the bell above the door and looked up at it.

"You have a good drive there, Mr. California veggie man," Jumper said.

Barbie looked through the pass-through and yelled out, "Come back when you can stay a while. I ain't engaged to him no more either."

"I will. Thanks again," I said, sticking my hand up high in a backward wave as I walked away without looking back.

Back on the road, I watched for the place where I had gotten onto the freeway earlier that day. I couldn't find it. I saw an eighteen-wheeler stopped at a turnout. I was sure it was the same dark green Freightliner I'd seen when I got back to the car that morning.

The driver was climbing down from behind the tractor. I was certain he was the same man who waved at me. I pulled the car over, jumped out, and ran across the freeway to greet him.

"Hi," I said.

"How ya doin'?" he replied, shooting me a suspicious look. "Can I help you?"

I detected his East Coast accent, maybe New York or New Jersey.

"Have you been here a long time?"

"Spent the night, from about 1:00 AM."

"Do you remember waving to me down there on the other side of you this morning?"

The truck driver's face twisted into a confused look. He looked in the direction of where I was saying I had been earlier.

"No, I don't think I've seen you before," he answered.

"Well, I was sure it was you," I said, walking around the rig to look down to where the car would have been.

The rocks looked as if they could have been the right place but there was no road and no freeway entrance.

"Well, maybe I haven't waken up yet," I said.

"How's that?"

"Oh, nothing. I got lost somewhere out here last night. I must have been at a different place along here."

"Sounds like you're still lost."

"Yeah, thanks."

I jogged back across the road to the car and got in. The motor was still running. I put it into gear and started driving home.

"Nobody's going to believe a word of this. I can't even find the place where I got off or back on the road. I don't even believe it myself."

"Then perhaps, human, you should have eaten the specialty at Jumper's," the recognizable voice of Big Frog sounded inside my head.

I was startled.

"Hey, where are you? Why did you all leave me this morning?"

"I am where I have been," he said. "We did not leave you. It was time for you to leave the gorge."

"But, the Great Meeting. What happened? I was looking forward to going."

"You had your Great Meeting. Our encounter was a success and our promise was kept."

The frog's words made me suddenly recall the brief encounter with my own reflection at the pond, and my last words there.

I repeated aloud, "Teddy, I'm glad to meet you."

I laughed silently.

"For eons we have gathered in the gorge, preparing all who were willing for the Great Meeting. It is always and only the meeting that wants to occur. Your experience is complete for now," the frog said.

"For now?" I asked. "What does that mean?"

"What does it mean indeed? You were prepared. The Great Meeting did occur on the twenty-third day, as was foretold. The purpose was fulfilled. You reclaimed that which was long lost. You now return to the world of humans with the reflection and the means. We have enjoyed our twenty-three days with you."

"But, it hasn't been twenty-three days. I checked. I got lost last night and it is the next day. It's been one day."

"Yes, one day for you, and a lifetime in our world. The world of possibility has no measure of time other than what we say."

"I wanted to say bye to everyone."

"Why would you say bye to us?"

"Because it was time to leave. I'm going to miss you."

"Human friend, I fear that you have missed the lesson of being with us," Big Frog said to me. "You have left the place where you joined us. You have not left us and we have not left you. You carry the reflection with you."

More of Big Frog's riddles made my head swim with dizzying thoughts. I knew then that the dream must not yet be over. I was certain I was going to awaken to find that my head had been severely damaged from that bump after all, and the car did wash away, and I would never find my way back to the world.

I drove on in silence. An hour or so later, I dropped my hand from the steering wheel to my abdomen. I felt something in my sweatshirt pocket. It was the stuffed frog. I pulled it out and set it on the dash.

"The reflection," I thought. "This stuffed frog must be the reflection."

I turned on the radio and did not think about the frogs again on the drive home.

At home, I told my wife the whole story. I knew she was going to think I had lost my mind. She did. She also said that might be a good thing to have lost, and told me that she could see something different in me. There was a new level of calmness and confidence now that she had not seen in me before. She liked it.

We talked for a long time, and we fell in love all over again. That night we went on a date back to the little restaurant. I ordered the same sandwich, and this time I enjoyed every bite of it.

A few days later, my older brother, Ben, came over for dinner. We reminisced about growing up together. We talked about the long drives in the mountains that we used to go on with our dad. I avoided saying anything about my recent experience, out of fear that he would have something judgmental to say if I told him I had spent twenty-three days talking to a group of frogs.

As we were clearing away the dishes from the table, Ben caught sight of the stuffed frog on the shelf above the television.

"Hey, you got another one of those," he said.

"What do you mean?" I asked him.

"That frog. It's just like the one you lost."

"What?"

"You don't remember? It was that time we went out for a drive with Pa looking for a fishin' hole. You were about six or seven. We were up in the mountains, and we got lost in the fog. Somehow, we got off the road and the car was stuck. We ended up walking through a big crack in the rocks and found this great big gorge. You would have thought old Pappy was a mule the way he could find a water hole. You had that darned old frog, just like that one. There were thousands of real frogs in that gorge too. It was pretty danged weird. I remember you and me playing with some pollywogs in a big pond there. We climbed up to a real nice grassy meadow, and that's where I think you lost your frog. You didn't want to leave until we found it, but Pa said we had to go before it got dark."

"Now that is weird," I said. "That was in the mountains in Arizona?"

"No, it was somewheres up there around Bass Lake. It was real strange. We were driving the back way out of Millerton. We went fishin' up at Kings River, but the trout and bass weren't takin' anything, not even my old trusty yellow rooster-tail. Only darned bites I was gettin' were those darned mosquitoes.

"Pappy said, 'Let's go for a drive,' and we did. I've never been able to find that place again. I've been all over those darned hills since then."

"Yeah, well I don't know if I can believe a word you say," I told him. "That yellow rooster-tail was mine. Mr. Williams gave it to me. I've told you that about a million times."

We both laughed, and then I told him about my recent trip. I told him what happened in the gorge, and how I had found the frog in the rocks coming down from the meadow. He listened to everything.

"Well," he said when I finished. "That frog looks like the same one."

"I'm sure it is the one," I said. "I remember hiding it, but where I found it was definitely in Arizona, somewhere just before Seligman along the 40. I remember Big Frog saying I carried 'the reflection' with me. My frog's name was Shadow. A shadow might be considered a kind of a reflection."

"Okay," Ben said. "I believe you. And I gotta get goin' here."

He started toward the door and turned to hug my wife.

"Louisie," he said. "If you see him start talkin' to that stuffed frog, you better get him over to the clinic quick."

He opened the door and walked outside.

"I will," she replied. "And you'd better get home. If it gets any foggier out there you might end up in that gorge tonight yourself."

We all laughed as the door shut behind him. I was holding the stuffed frog and pointed it at Louise. I did my best attempt at ventriloquism.

"Watch your step, woman. Your husband was chosen by us frogs."

      ❦   ❦   ❦

It has been a long time since my curious adventure in the gorge of the Master Frogs. I've had no further communication with the frogs as yet, but I know there was a reason for my being summoned there.

I am certain that when the time is right, when I am prepared enough, or maybe when I am not so prepared, the real purpose of the Great Meeting will manifest.

In the meantime, I share the lessons I learned with other people. I do my best to prepare them for their own Great Meetings, and for the time when humans will come out of the darkness and make the world whole again.

THE END

0-595-27383-1